KATY PIS

THE PALOMINO

Pacific Press® Publishing Association
Nampa, Idaho
Oshawa, Ontario, Canada
www.pacificpress.com

Edited by Jerry D. Thomas
Designed by Dennis Ferree
Cover art by Douglas C. Klauba

Additional copies of this book may be purchased at
http://www.adventistbookcenter.com

Library of Congress Cataloging-in-Publication Data:

Pistole, Katy, 1963-
The palomino / Katy Pistole.
p. cm.— (The Sonrise farm series)
Summary: After putting Jesus first in her life, Jenny finds that working at a horse farm leads her to her heart's desire.
ISBN 0-8163-1863-8
[1. Horses 2. Horse farms 3. Christian life 4.Virginia]
I.Title II. Series.

PZ7.P64265 Pal 2002
dc21 2001036370

02 03 04 05 06 • 5 4 3 2

Contents

Dedication

To my Mom, Judy Thomsen.

You always told me I should write.
Thank you for the years of warm encouragement
and discipleship. I love you.

Trust in the Lord and do good;
dwell in the land and enjoy safe pasture.
Delight yourself in the Lord
and he will give you the desires of your heart.
Psalm 37:3, 4 (NIV)

Jenny Thomas raced the Palomino stallion up the hill. She rode bareback and without a bridle, her blond hair tangling with his silver mane as she clung to his golden neck. At the crest of the hill, she turned him and they stood gazing over the meadow below. Horse and girl breathed as one, drinking the cool morning air. Tendrils of steam rose from the stallion's flared nostrils and trickled away into the mist.

Ring . . . ring . . . The shrill of the telephone pierced the stillness, jerking Jenny out of her meadow and back into bed. She sat up, staring at her clenched hands, almost expecting to find strands of silvery mane dangling from them. They were empty. Jenny flopped back into the downy pillow and squeezed her blue eyes tight, hoping to recapture the elusive horse.

It wasn't going to work. She could hear the sparrows squabbling on her window sill and shower water swooshing through the pipes. Early spring sun pushed through the blinds, spilling shimmery dapples into every corner of her room.

Jenny stretched and yawned as she blinked the sleep from her eyes. Twirling a lock of blond hair around her finger, she peered about the room. Her breath caught. There it was.

Sometimes, early in the morning, Jenny's favorite poster caught the sunlight in a wondrous way. It was a Palomino stal-

lion loping across a field. Rippling sunbeams danced on his gold hide as he ran. She could almost *see* movement. *I have got to get hold of my imagination,* she thought, blinking hard. Clouds passed over the sun, destroying the illusion.

Jenny heaved a sigh as she curled up under her quilt. Then it came back. *Horse camp! How many days until horse camp?* She flew to her desk. "Today is Friday," she murmured, twisting her hair. "Forty-seven days to go." Her hand trembled with excitement as she crossed another day off the calendar.

"G' morning, Mom," Jenny greeted, plunking down on her chair in the tiny kitchen.

Jenny's dad followed close behind, his usually tan face, pale.

"Mike, what is it?" Mrs. Thomas gasped.

Mr. Thomas clung to the back of a kitchen chair like a drowning man, "That was Josh Moore on the phone." He sank into the chair.

"The owner of your construction company?" Mrs. Thomas whispered, hand over her mouth, as if she didn't want to say the words.

Mr. Thomas nodded. "Josh's partner cleaned him out. Stole all the money. Josh is broke. He owes more than his machinery is worth. He can't even pay me for the last two weeks."

"What'll we do?" Mrs. Thomas cried.

Mr. Thomas buried his blond head in his hands. "I don't know!"

A cold knife of fear stabbed Jenny's heart. "Dad, what about horse camp?" He looked up and she saw the answer in his eyes. "I knew it!" she screamed, fleeing the room. She buried her hot face in the cool pillow, "God," she sobbed, "if You didn't want me to go to horse camp, why did You let me get all excited about it?"

Why did Dad have to lose his job? Why did we have to come

here in the first place? We moved because of Dad's great job offer. Yeah, great. I miss North Carolina. I miss summers with Cousin Leah on her horse farm. Nobody even has horses around here. It's too expensive. The only good thing that happened here in Virginia was horse camp, and now that's gone.

Maybe we'll go back, she thought. The only person she'd miss would be Tessa, and maybe her elderly neighbor Mrs. Grant.

Someone knocked softly.

"Come in," she grumbled.

Mr. Thomas peeked around the door. "Hi, Sweetheart. Are you OK?"

"Fine," she huffed.

He sat on the edge of her bed and tried to pull her close. She stiffened her shoulders. *This is all your fault,* her brain shrieked.

"Jenny, I don't know where to start."

"How about, 'We're moving back to North Carolina.' "

"Jenny, you know we can't do that."

"Why not," she yelled. "I didn't want to come here in the first place. I'll never get to ride again."

"Look Jen, I'm sorry, really sorry. I didn't choose to lose my job. I don't understand why this has happened now, but I do know that God is in charge and that He brought us to Virginia for a reason. I'm scared too, but I believe that He will take care of us. Will you pray with me right now?"

"No," she sighed, suddenly feeling exhausted. "I need to get ready for school." She pulled herself upright and began rummaging through her closet. When she turned around, he had slipped out. Her soul felt as empty as her room.

The sky had opened and rain cascaded down her windows. The brief moment of sunlight had disappeared as quickly as her happiness. She thought about the day ahead. She still had to go to school—that place where she had no place. Would

she ever fit in? She sucked in a deep breath and pulled out her blue dress. Her dad *always* told her how beautiful her eyes looked when she wore it.

"Like cornflowers, Jenny," he would grin, mussing her hair. She could use a compliment from Dad right about now.

"Mom, Dad, where are you?" Jen's voice echoed in the empty kitchen.

"Here, Jenny, at the back door. Come and wave goodbye to your dad. He's heading out to talk to Mr. Moore."

But he was already backing out of the driveway and didn't see her raised hand. She had to bite her lip *hard* to stop the tears. *How will I get through this day?* She wondered.

The bus turned a hard left and Jenny had to grab the seat bar in front of her to avoid landing in Tessa's lap.

"I'll just get my mom to pay your way," Tessa shrugged.

"I can't do that," Jenny retorted to her best friend, pulling herself upright,

"Why not?" asked Tessa, tossing her dark curls. "It's only $200."

"$200!" Jenny gasped. "I had no idea it was so much. Well, it doesn't matter. My folks would never let me take money from a friend."

"You could work it off," Tessa suggested. "You could clean my room."

"No thanks," replied Jenny, gazing through the window. "But that gives me an idea." She pitched her plan at dinner that night. Mom stopped chewing and placed her fork on the plate. Dad raised his eyebrows in surprise.

"Mom, Dad, if I raise the money for camp, can I go?"

"Jenny, do you have any idea how much money we're talking about?" inquired Dad.

"It's $200. Right?"

"Right," they harmonized.

"Well, I'll mow lawns or baby-sit or clean people's houses."

Mom and Dad glanced at each other, then back at Jenny.

Jenny could hear the wall clock behind her, ticking, louder, louder, louder. Finally, Dad cleared his throat.

"Well," he said softly, reaching for her hand. "I think it's a great idea. I don't know if you'll be able to pull it off, but I'm sure proud of you for trying."

Ahhh. It felt good to breathe again. Jen hadn't realized she was holding her breath.

"I'll make an announcement at church, if you want," Dad smiled. "Two workers for hire."

"And I will help you make some flyers, if you want to post them at the grocery store," said Mom.

This will work, thought Jenny, imagining lazy afternoons playing with adorable babies.

Her first job was to mow Mrs. Grant's lawn. "I heard about your predicament, and I'd like to help," chirped the cheerful old voice on the phone. "Come over to my house tomorrow morning. How does $10 sound?"

"Great," responded Jenny with vigor. "I'll see you in the morning."

Jenny had never noticed that Mrs. Grant's yard was the size of a plantation. She finished mowing and raking at 12:47 P.M. It was more than three and a half hours of backbreaking labor.

Jenny placed her first precious ten-dollar bill inside the front flap of her Bible. *Only $190 more to go.* She curled up on her bed, just for a moment.

The stallion trumpeted as she approached. Then he charged. She stood motionless, unafraid. The ground shuddered as he thundered closer. He skidded to a halt. She grabbed a handful of silvery mane and leapt onto his back. The big horse reared and whirled away.

"Jeneeee, dinner," Mom called.

She woke, confused by the darkness of her room. Had she slept all afternoon? Her shoulders ached. Her head felt thick. *Am I going to be able to do this?* she wondered.

Church was something they always did in the Thomas household. Jenny fidgeted as she tried to pay attention to Pastor Jeff. She heard something about Jesus, but her brain kept jumping back to horses and camp. What kind of horse would she ride? Would it be a Palomino?

Pastor Jeff allowed Mr. Thomas to stand and make his announcement, just before prayer time.

"I'm sure many of you know our situation," Dad said, looking uncomfortable. His big, callused hands were clenching and unclenching. "We are praying that I will find another job soon. We are also trying to find a way for Jenny to get to horse camp. Jenny, stand up please."

She felt the hot blush burn through to her hair roots. She glanced at Pastor Jeff, who smiled kindly, eyes crinkling at the corners.

"Jenny," Dad continued, placing his arm around her shoulder, "is looking for baby-sitting, lawn mowing, or cleaning chores. She is a hard worker. If anyone needs these services, please consider Jenny."

Jen gave a stiff wave and a grin, then plunked down into her seat. *Whew, at least that's over,* she thought.

After church, Jenny's parents discussed the sermon as they

began their traditional afternoon drive. The destinations of these drives were secret and always fun. Jenny sprawled out over the back seat, staring through the window at the rows of houses. *How I wish we could live in the country. I could get a horse* . . . The voices of her folks faded as her daydream unfolded.

Suddenly, Jen's eyes focused. They were driving past a huge equestrian park. The park was an impressive 100-acre expanse on the outskirts of town. The big green sign usually said HUNTER'S RIDGE, but was covered by a temporary sign that announced: JUMPER SHOW TODAY. Jenny feverishly rolled down her window, straining to see.

She caught Dad's smiling blue eyes in the rear view mirror. The car slowed. Dad clicked the left turn signal. After an oncoming car passed, they pulled into the driveway of the park. Stones clunked against the bottom of the station wagon as they crept down the dusty gravel drive.

Jenny stared at the three outdoor rings on the left, then straight ahead at the huge indoor arena. There were five barns on the right and two smaller barns behind the first outdoor ring. All the buildings were painted deep red. Behind the indoor arena was a cross-country course with jumps through the woods and fields. "What a place," she whispered.

The parking lot looked full, but Dad squeezed into a spot. The three of them started toward the outdoor rings. There were horses and trailers everywhere. Riders rushed about in britches, shouting instructions to their helpers. Horses whinnied and jerked impatiently at their lead ropes.

Jenny heard the metallic clank of a horseshoe meeting a trailer door. The air was filled with the intoxicating fragrance of horse sweat and hay. Next to the indoor arena stood a snack bar. The aroma of French fries wafted onto the breeze making Jen's mouth water.

They found a large dogwood tree to sit under and watch

several rounds of stadium jumping. Jenny scooted close to the ring and sat spellbound, arms locked around her knees.

Her muscles tensed as a big black horse approached the last jump. *Wait, wait. Now!* The horse burst upward at the perfect moment. He landed and the jump stayed up. Jenny had to catch her breath. Her eyes stung. *Blink, you ninny,* she chided herself.

Dad stood up and stretched. "I'm starved, let's get home and eat lunch." A glance at her wrist told her that they had sat there for over an hour. It had passed in moments.

Mom extended her arms and moaned, "Jenny, help me up. My legs are stuck." Jenny pulled, giggling at the thought. They walked in silence to the car, brushing their hands together to get rid of the red clay dust.

I don't know how yet, but I am going to do this, Jen determined.

Jenny's vision of lazy afternoons sitting with adorable babies quickly blurred. She found herself surrounded instead by drippy noses and endless untied shoelaces. Her weekends were spent mowing and raking. Evenings were taken up with homework.

She rushed home after her last exam and counted the wad of bills in her Bible. Ninety-four dollars. Less than half of what she needed. She eyed the calendar. *Two weeks left. There is no way.*

After dinner, the phone rang. Both Jenny and Dad leapt to answer it. Dad won.

"Mike Thomas speaking. Yes, she's here." He handed her the receiver slowly, grinning at her impatient dance.

"Hello," she answered breathlessly.

"Hello, Jenny. This is Mrs. Harris. I'm the nursery supervisor at church. I need an assistant during the women's Bible study. It would be from 9:00 to 12:00 on Tuesdays and Thursdays. The church can pay you three dollars an hour, plus a free-will offering from the moms. I can't give you a dollar amount because it depends on how many little ones you have. Can you help me out? I could pick you up on my way?"

Jenny imagined being tied up and run over by ten or twenty screaming banshees. Then she saw herself at horse camp cantering smoothly in a ring. She squeezed her eyes shut, grimacing. "Sure, I'd love to," she lilted, artificially sweet. *What a hypocrite I am,* she thought, hanging up.

"What was that about?" inquired Dad.

"Another baby-sitting job," Jenny groaned. "This is much harder than I thought it would be."

Dad smiled at her, patting the couch next to him. She snuggled into his warm side. He mussed her hair. "Nothing good comes easily," he said softly. "Jenny, have you been giving something to the Lord from your earnings?"

She pulled away and stared at him. "How can I give when I don't even have enough for camp?" *Surely he is joking!*

He wasn't. "Luke 6, verse 38, says, ' "Give, and it will be given to you. A good measure, pressed down, shaken together and running over, will be poured into your lap. For with the measure you use, it will be measured to you" ' " (NIV).

"Daaad," she groaned. "Do I have to? I am never going to make enough if I have to give it away."

"Jenny, this is between you and God. You are old enough to decide what is right. I am not going to tell you what to do."

Great, she thought. *A guilt trip.*

"Pray about it," he continued, "And remember, we all love you."

She kissed his cheek. "I'll see you in the morning. I guess I'm working in the nursery tomorrow. I need my rest."

He squeezed her tight. "Goodnight, sweetheart. I am proud of your hard work."

Jenny tossed and turned before nodding off. She kept thinking about giving up her hard-earned money. It wasn't fair.

There were fifteen screaming banshees in the nursery on

Tuesday. She was paid $9.00 by the church and $10.00 by the moms. That brought her grand total to $113.00.

Thursday was almost as bad. By the weekend, she had collected $130. Minus $13. *This isn't right,* she thought as she sat next to her dad in church. *God wouldn't want me to give up this money. I'm in a desperate situation.* Dad placed his envelope in the plate and sat back. Jenny placed her wad of cash in the plate and sat back. *I was so close.*

Pastor Jeff preached about having a cheerful heart. Jenny squirmed, feeling anything but cheerful. All she could think about was the $117 remaining in her possession. And she would have to give again next week! She still needed $83. She could never earn that in one week.

Tuesday she brought in $20 more. Thursday the collection from the moms contained $50! Her grand total by Friday was $187.

She was due to mow Mrs. Grant's field that afternoon. That would be $197. *Minus $19 after church,* her heart complained. She would be back down to $178. *I may as well give up now,* she thought. *If I hadn't given that money away . . .*

She mowed anyway, unable to quit trying. Mrs. Grant wasn't even home to pay her. She walked home, stooped and dejected. She was ready to tell her folks that she had failed. "Dad," she began at dinner. "I, I didn't . . ." tears flooded her eyes and her throat closed.

Ding Dong. The doorbell rang.

"I'll get it," Mom said.

Jenny stared at her bowl of soup. Her stomach was churning, her mouth paralyzed. She heard her mother's voice. Loud and excited. "Thank you, Mrs. Grant. I'll tell her." Mom rushed back to the table. "Mrs. Grant says that some young man came around looking for work. He told her that anyone who mowed that lawn for less than $15 was either stupid or desperate."

Mom held out a stack of bills. "Mrs. Grant says she owes you some back pay. Count it, Jen."

Jenny took the money from her mother's hand. She counted it in a daze. Thirty-five dollars. That brought her total to $222. Ten percent was $22. After giving she would be left with $200 . . . exactly.

Tears streamed down her face. She looked up into her father's eyes. He was crying with her. "Thank you, Mrs. Grant," she whispered.

June 17th—horse camp day—arrived hot and humid. Jenny's stomach started doing gymnastics the moment her eyes snapped open. The family ate breakfast together, though Jenny could barely swallow her French toast.

"Jenny, you are going to need your energy. Eat your breakfast." Mom chided.

With that, Jenny's appetite appeared and she cleaned her plate. She helped clear the table, then scampered to her room to change. The brochure had specified comfortable pants and shoes with a heel. *I'll wear black stretch pants and leather work boots,* she decided. Glancing in her full-length mirror, Jenny was pleased with what she saw. She felt ready to conquer the world. She rushed back to the kitchen where Mom handed her a brown paper lunch bag and some carrots.

"Those are for your new friends," Mom said with a wink.

"Thanks!" Jenny grinned and grabbed the bag and carrots. She flew down the front stairs to the driveway and leapt into the front seat of the station wagon. "Come on, Mom," she shouted, her hands shaking as she buckled the seat belt.

Mom marched out briskly, puffing a little. "Sorry," she

apologized, "just grabbing some last-minute things." She dumped her suitcase-sized purse in the back seat, then handed Jenny the camp flyer. Jen flipped it over to read the directions.

"OK," Jenny said, reading fast, "here is the red gate on the left and the white board fence on the right, we should be able to see the sign . . . It should be coming up on the right . . . Ahh, here! Turn here, Mom!" she shrieked.

"Jenny! Please don't scream!" Mom sputtered, slamming on the brakes. As they rounded the turn, Jenny noticed the big hanging sign—Sonrise Farm.

"Look, Mom, they misspelled sunrise." She turned the camp flyer back over to read the front. It was spelled the same way. Jenny had never noticed it before.

Mom turned her head to read it. When she turned back she had a funny smile on her face. "Jenny, that sign is not misspelled. This is an answer to prayer."

The car continued up the driveway, while Jenny reflected on what Mom had said. She thought about the money. *Could God really be interested in my horseback riding?* she wondered. *And could He really be making this possible for me?*

"Here we are," Mom announced. Jenny's eyes focused on the barns and the other cars. She craned her neck searching for Tessa. There she was. "Oh, no!" Jenny gasped. "I can't stay here."

Jen stared in dismay. Everyone else was wearing real riding britches and tall black boots! Even Tessa was decked out, looking like a pro. Jenny wanted to leave and never come back. *What about all my hard work?* she thought

Mom recognized her expression, and reached over to gently cup Jenny's chin in her hand. "Jennifer Lynne," she whispered, looking deep into Jen's teary eyes. "This is your decision. I just want you to remember that you are a child of God, and you are as good as anyone here. If you want to go home,

I'll take you, but I think you should get out there and show them what you are made of!"

Jenny nodded. She gave her mom a watery, chin-shaking smile. Taking a deep breath, she reached for the door.

"Wait, Jenny. Dad and I want you to have this," Mom reached into the back seat and grabbed a large wrapped box.

Jenny stared at the box in her lap for about one second. She tore the paper off in one big piece and opened the top. She couldn't breathe. Inside was a black velvet helmet. Not a cheap, velveteen one, but a deep, rich black, velvet helmet. She placed it on her head and tried to buckle it, but her hands were shaking. Mom reached over and clicked the buckle. A perfect fit!

"Mom, thank you so much, and please thank Daddy too. It's beautiful. I love it." Jenny hugged her mom, then climbed out of the car. *I will show these girls,* she promised herself. Gritting her teeth, she started toward the group.

"Ooh, are you one of the stable hands?" laughed a sarcastic voice.

Jenny rolled her eyes. *Here we go,* she thought

Tessa sidled over, "Gosh, Jenny, why did you dress like such a geek? I'm not sure I can hang out with you today."

That hurt. Jenny opened her mouth to retort, but was cut off by another voice.

"Ladies, may I have your attention? My name is Kathy O'Riley. I will be your instructor for the next week. Please listen to me at all times. Everything I tell you is important."

Jenny forgot about Tessa and everyone else as she listened to her instructor. She felt like pinching herself; she was listening to her *instructor!*

The girls headed up toward the barn, with Jenny first in line. As they approached the big yellow barn, Jenny heard one of the girls scream. "Oooh . . . **gross!** I just stepped in a huge pile of poop."

Kathy turned around. "All right. Our first lesson has begun. Horses are dirty. For all you ladies who think that we are just going to be riding, please be assured that we will also be mucking out stalls, grooming, and doing other chores. Horses are large animals, and they create *large* manure piles. If this bothers you, please watch where you put your feet!"

Wow, thought Jenny happily, *this is going to be even better than I thought.*

The morning passed quickly for Jenny, though by lunchtime everyone else seemed hot and cranky. Jenny relaxed against a shady crabapple tree, eating her peanut butter and jelly sandwich. She watched the school horses eat their hay and wondered which one she would ride. There wasn't a single Palomino in the barn, but Jenny didn't care.

Tessa limped over and sank down beside her. She nibbled a bit of her tuna salad, then whimpered, "Jenny … I … I'm sorry I was so mean to you this morning."

Jenny glanced at her friend's sweaty face and smiled. " It's OK, Tessa. Anyway, I bet I'm more comfortable than you are right now."

Tessa's smile was a painful grimace. "I'll trade you my riding boots for those comfortable work boots. You would not believe how big my blisters are."

"Sorry," Jenny replied. "I'll stick with my tried and true. Oh, Tessa, your beautiful blouse, it's trashed."

"I know," shrugged Tessa. "I don't really care about it anyway."

The girls finished their lunch, chatting and giggling about the morning. A piercing whistle from Kathy interrupted them. Jenny jumped up and threw her lunch bag into the large green trashcan.

"Oh, Jenny, help me up," Tessa moaned. Jenny obligingly gave her a hand and watched sympathetically as Tessa stood hunched, rubbing her back. "I'm so sore and I haven't even ridden yet."

Jenny was suddenly thankful for all those hours of mowing lawns and lifting children. Her back was strong, and she was ready to go!

Jenny's horse was a stocky chestnut gelding with a star in the middle of his forehead. His full name was Second Chance Charlie, because Kathy had bought him off of the meat wagon. His barn name was Chance, and Jenny was delighted to meet him. She patted his thick red neck while leading him to the fence rail.

Tessa's mount was a large black Welsh pony named Ebony. Ebony had a sweet delicate face, but wild eyes. She emerged from her stall looking around like a frightened deer. In spite of Ebony's frantic appearance, she was a quiet, lazy pony—according to Kathy. Tessa looked unconvinced.

The girls learned how to tie a safety knot and began grooming their mounts. By the time Jenny had used the curry comb, Tessa had finished grooming Ebony.

"How did you do that so fast?" asked Jenny.

Kathy appeared behind them. "She is not finished. Let me show you," she said patiently. She took the curry comb from Jenny's box and demonstrated how to use it to get out the trapped dirt. By the time Tessa *really* finished grooming Ebony, she was a sweaty mess from the effort. Meanwhile, Jenny had learned how to tighten the girth and was placing the bit in Chance's mouth.

The group headed to the ring leading their horses. Kathy stood in the center of the ring and asked Jenny to bring Chance to her. Kathy took the reins from Jenny and demonstrated the correct way to mount and dismount. Then she asked Jenny to try.

Jenny placed her foot in the stirrup, gave a small hop, and in one fluid motion mounted perfectly. She stared down at a grinning Kathy.

"Well done, Jenny. You're a natural."

* * *

The rest of the day flew by, and Jenny felt more and more comfortable on Chance. She was oblivious to anyone but Kathy. She listened intently to her instructions and before long was stopping and turning Chance every time she wanted to.

Jen happened to look up and see poor Tessa trying to stop Ebony. The black pony was marching back toward the barn. Tessa's hands were near her ears pulling the reins. Kathy had to walk over and lead Ebony back to the group. Tessa shot Jenny an agonized look. Before Jenny knew it, it was time to go back to the barn and learn how to untack the horses. Tessa groaned when Kathy explained that she had to groom Ebony *again* after riding.

Jenny dismounted and hugged Chance's sturdy neck, burying her face in his mane. It was the sweetest smell. She removed the saddle and bridle, carefully brushing all saddle traces away. When she finished, he was sleek and shiny again.

The girls gave their horses a couple of carrots. Ebony bit Tessa's finger by accident, so Kathy demonstrated the correct way to feed treats with a flat palm. Jenny led Chance back to his stall and patted his neck. "Thanks for a great ride," she whispered. Chance blew through his nose and whickered for his dinner.

Kathy gave a few closing remarks about the day's instructions, and then the girls were free to sit and relax on the lawn until their folks came to retrieve them. Most of the girls complained loudly about their feet and legs. Tessa sat hunched and embarrassed. Jenny felt tired, but exhilarated. When her mom drove up and blew the horn, she raced to the car, threw the door open, and sat breathless for a moment.

"Well," Mom queried, "how was it?"

Jenny almost burst. "It was incredible!" She was still gushing when they pulled into the driveway. Dad grinned with delight at Jen's description of the day.

"Jen, come and sit with us," he invited, patting the empty spot on the sofa. "I got a job today. And not just a job, but a contracting business of my own. Josh Moore contacted the president of a bank that we remodeled. They are willing to give me a business loan. It will be kind of tight at first, but Josh gave me his client phonebook and I already have some good leads."

Jenny stared at her dad then gave a delighted whoop and danced around the room. *What an awesome day,* her heart sang.

Jenny lay in bed the next morning, debating the best way to get up. She felt like she'd been run over by a Clydesdale. She concluded, after several attempts, that there wasn't a painless way to do it.

She bit her lip and sat up. Everything ached. She shuffled gingerly into the kitchen. Mom took one look at her and diagnosed the problem. "Jenny, take a couple of Tylenol and a warm bath with Epsom salts. It'll fix you right up."

"OK, Mom," she croaked. When she cut her waffles, even her wrists hurt. The maple syrup bit her tongue with sharp sweetness. "Great waffles," she mumbled stickily, reaching for her third one.

The bath and medicine worked. She felt like a new person afterwards. Mom was so smart.

They pulled into the driveway of Sonrise Farm. Jenny clambered out of the car and jogged to the meeting place. It was deserted. Mom got out of the car and waited with her, just to make sure everything was all right. After a few minutes Kathy emerged from the lower barn and strolled over to meet them.

"You must be Jenny's mom," she smiled, extending her hand. "I'm Kathy, the instructor. It's so nice to meet you."

"Yes, Kathy," smiled Mom, accepting Kathy's hand. "Jenny told me all about her wonderful time here yesterday."

Kathy scanned the empty yard and declared, "Well, it looks as if my only student is here. I'll bet everyone else is too sore."

No way! Jenny thought. This was too incredible. She was going to spend the day alone with Kathy and the horses. Heaven had arrived!

"Well then," smiled Mom, "I will leave you two alone to do your thing. Jenny, I'll pick you up at five o'clock. Do you have your lunch?"

"Right here, Mom," she confirmed, waving the paper bag. "Bye, see ya."

* * *

The morning passed in the swish of a tail. Jenny rode Chance, Ebony, and another school horse named Jack. She learned how to trot and post and helped Kathy prepare the lunch feed. She mucked out three stalls and picked the school horses' feet. She relished every moment, even mucking out the stalls. Jenny and Kathy ate lunch together under the crabapple tree talking horses the entire time.

The rest of the day was like a dream for Jenny. She rode three more school horses, and she picked up posting so well that Kathy allowed her to canter. She was on a cute bay Morgan named Little Joe, who, Kathy warned her, could be feisty.

Jenny started well at the trot, then loosened the reins a little. She gave him a squeeze with her legs and they were cantering! It was lovely, just as she had known it would be. They made one loop around the ring. It wasn't until Jen tried to slow him that she realized Little Joe was pounding faster and faster around the ring. She heard Kathy shouting at her from what sounded like miles away. "Keep your heels down, and *pull him up!*"

It really was like floating, and she wasn't frightened at all. Suddenly she *was* floating for a second, then she was free falling. Somehow Jen had lost the horse, or he had lost her. The floating sensation was rudely interrupted as she landed, *kerplop,* on her rear end. She sat stunned for a moment, then started giggling. Kathy sprinted toward her.

"Jenny. Are you all right?" Kathy shouted from several feet away.

"I'm OK, I think," Jen replied unbuckling her helmet. She felt hot and giddy.

"Well, that was thrilling!" Kathy said with a chuckle. "How do you feel? Do you want to get back up on Little Joe and show him who is boss?"

Jenny didn't really *want* to, but she had heard somewhere that you need to get back on a horse after it has dumped you. She stood up, brushed the blue stone dust from the seat of her pants, placed her helmet back on her head, and mounted.

Whoa, it seems much higher this time, she thought looking at the hard ground below. Kathy jogged to the side of the ring and grabbed a long piece of webbing. It looked like a long dog leash.

"What's that?" inquired Jenny.

"This is a lunge line," explained Kathy clipping the buckle to Little Joe's bit. "Basically it's a very long rein that allows me to stand in the middle of the ring and hold on to your horse so you can figure out how the brakes work."

That makes sense, thought Jenny. She squeezed Little Joe and he broke into a trot. Then she squeezed him again and he began cantering. Kathy made her trot, canter, and then trot again for about thirty minutes until Jenny's legs were jelly. Finally, Kathy removed the lunge line and asked Jenny to try cantering on her own.

She walked Little Joe around the ring once, then squeezed him into a trot. "Heels down. Heels down," Jenny whispered to herself. *There is just so much to remember!* She listened for Kathy's instructions.

"You look good. Keep those heels down. Now ask him for the canter as you approach the corner. Use your outside leg. Great! Now sit down with it. Feel the three beat time?"

I'm cantering! Her heart pounded in the same rhythm. It just felt *right.* She and Little Joe cantered smoothly twice around.

"Trot." Kathy shouted. "Time to slow down, daredevil."

Jenny nodded her assent. *Now how do I do this?* She pushed her heels down, sat deep in the saddle and pulled back on the reins.

The frisky horse snaked his head, then let out a buck! Now her heart was pounding *way* faster than they were cantering. She sat down again and pulled. Little Joe shook his head and muscled it down to buck again. Instinctively, Jenny kicked him and gave one hard jerk on the reins.

Little Joe stopped so fast that Jenny wound up on his neck. She quickly shimmied back down and settled in the saddle. She squeezed and got a trot, squeezed again and got a canter. Jenny pulled him up and got a trot. "Good boy," she crowed patting his sweaty neck. She was breathing as heavily as he was.

Kathy jogged over, "That was great, Jenny, you really handled him like a natural horsewoman."

They walked back to the barn together and Kathy helped untack Little Joe. The day was nearly over and the excitement left Jenny feeling drained. She realized with a sick feeling that the week was nearly half over. Tomorrow was Wednesday and camp was over on Friday. Then it was back to a horseless life.

How could she become a great horsewoman if all she ever did was ride once a year? She did not have the money to go to camp all summer, and they couldn't afford to own a horse. Especially now.

Jenny heard Mom's car crunching the gravel in the driveway.

She flopped into the front seat with an enormous sigh. Mom looked her over for a moment, then said bluntly, "Tomorrow is Wednesday. Camp is almost half over, isn't it?" Jenny regarded her mother for a moment, amazed. She could feel hot

tears throbbing like a roaring river behind her eyes. If they started, there would be no stopping them. Ever.

She stared at her dirty hands folded limply in her lap. Finally, she whispered brokenly, "Mom, today Kathy told me that I am a natural horsewoman. I can't go to camp all summer and I don't even know anyone else who has a horse. What kind of a horsewoman can I be if I don't ride horses?

They didn't say very much after that, and Mom didn't push her to speak. The car pulled into the driveway, then lurched to a stop. Jenny jumped out and ran to her room. She closed her door quietly, then curled up on the middle of her bed. She felt exhausted from the day and was soon sleeping soundly. She awoke to a gentle knock.

"Come in," she mumbled. It was Dad. He sat on the edge of her bed. "Hi," she croaked, sitting up. She cleared her throat, then gratefully guzzled the tall glass of juice he offered.

"Jenny, Mom tells me you're feeling really sad about horse camp." His big arms crushed her to him in a mighty bear hug. She heard his heart beat. *Lub Dub. Lub Dub.*

"Daddy," she sobbed. "I am having the best time in my whole life, and Kathy says I have natural talent, but I just don't see how I can ever use it. Camp will be over on Friday. We don't have the money for me to go anymore. It is so expensive—but I don't see how I can go back to how I was before."

Jenny looked up and realized that Dad's eyes were full of tears also. She felt a flash of shame. "Oh, Daddy, I didn't mean it . . . about the money," she sobbed.

Dad squeezed her close, "Jenny, I'm crying because I love you so much, it hurts me to see you so hurt. God loves you even more than I do, if that's possible. He loves you so much that he sent His only Son to die for you and for me. I'd like to read you something."

He went and got his worn leather Bible, opening it to Psalm 37. He began reading verse 3. " 'Trust in the Lord and

do good' " He read softly. " 'Delight yourself in the Lord and he will give you the desires of your heart.' "

Jenny placed her hand on Dad's arm, stopping him. "Dad, does that mean that if I just trust Him He will give me whatever I want?"

Dad smiled lovingly as he read verse 5, " 'Commit your way to the Lord; trust in him and he will do this.' Jenny, I believe these verses mean that if you trust in the Lord, He will be faithful and will make you desire good things—in other words, *He* will create the desires of your heart. God loves you so much, Jenny. You can go to Him with anything. Talk to Him about the horses, pray that He will change your heart if necessary."

Jenny leaned against her father's chest feeling his strength. Dad put his muscular arm around her and bowed his head in prayer. "Father, thank You that we can come to you with any troubles, great or small. We pray for Jenny today. We thank You for her enthusiasm and for her deep love for horses. We trust You, Lord, that You know everything about us. We give You this problem. I pray that Jenny will finish the week safely and with joy. Amen."

"Amen," whispered Jenny.

"Now let's get some dinner, I'm starving," exclaimed Dad tousling her sandy hair.

The next morning Jenny woke and sat up. She coiled her long blond hair around her finger as she thought about what Dad had said last night. She wondered if her heavenly Father really loved her in the way her earthly father said.

"Jesus," she whispered earnestly, "if You are really there and if You care, please let me know You."

Jenny greeted her parents with a cheery, "Good morning." She proceeded to load her fork with the scrambled eggs and potatoes.

As her mom dropped her off at Sonrise Farm, Jenny took a deep breath, deciding to have a great day. *I just won't think about next week,* she decided.

Most of the girls were back, complaining loudly. They limped around all day and even Tessa didn't get to trot long enough to learn how to post. Kathy asked Jenny to demonstrate, so Jenny spent her day helping to teach the other girls some of the things she had learned on Tuesday.

At lunch Tessa sat next to Jenny, eyeing her with new respect. "Jenny, why didn't you tell me you knew how to ride?"

Jenny looked at her, surprised. "I used to spend summers at my cousin's horse farm. This is just the first time I've had lessons."

"Well," replied Tessa, chewing slowly, "you must be a natural."

Jenny thought about what Tessa had said. Tessa was the second person in as many days to tell her that she was a natural. *Maybe I really am.*

Wednesday ended with Jenny on her knees beside her bed. She wasn't sure quite how she had gotten there. She remembered saying her prayers this way when she was a little girl.

"Dear Jesus, if You can really create the desires of my heart, please make them accept Your will. I love horses, I always have—but if this is not what You want for me, I need help to not want them. I trust You to come into my heart and make it Yours. Amen."

Jenny felt the tears swell, and she let them flow. She climbed under her covers thinking about the desperation of her prayer. *I have to give up the horses. There is just no other way. Anything else is torture.* She drew a deep ragged breath and allowed a wave of peace to sweep over her. The breath came out in a sigh as she fell asleep.

Morning came and Jenny's old friends, the sunbeams, were back. They played with the pictures on her walls, then caught the Palomino stallion, setting it aglow. She glanced at it and smiled. It was beautiful, but did not have the hypnotic power it once had.

Jen got up and padded into the kitchen. She was deep in thought when her mother placed pancakes in front of her. "Thanks, Mom," she smiled sheepishly. Jenny dressed for the barn and packed her lunch in a haze. She did notice that the drive to the barn seemed much shorter today.

"I've discovered a short cut," said Mom as she stopped in front of the house. "It's only about three miles from the house if we go this back way."

Jenny nodded vacantly as she climbed out. She wandered up to the yellow barn and began grooming Chance. She looked around at the other girls. Some were brushing correctly, but most were dropping their brushes or just barely touching the horse.

"Here, Kelly, let me help you with that," said Jenny. She showed Kelly how to put her hand under the strap of the brush and really use her arm to get dirt out of the hair. Jenny glanced up and caught Kathy observing. Kathy winked, thanking Jenny for her help.

Mom arrived at five o'clock and Jenny jogged down from

the barn to poke her head into the window of the station wagon. "Mom, come and see Chance. He's the horse I've been riding all week." Mom followed Jenny up the small hill to the big yellow barn. Chance was the third horse on the left. Jenny escorted Mom to the Dutch door, gave a regal bow and formally introduced them.

"Mother, this is Second Chance Charlie, also known as Chance. Chance, this is Mrs. Judith Thomas, also known as Mom." Jenny had accomplished the introduction without cracking a smile, but the girls, silly from the heat and hard work, burst out laughing. Jenny looked around giggling and again caught Kathy's eye. Kathy winked and grinned at Jenny once again.

Jenny and Mom climbed back into the car, talking about camp and ponies all the way home. "I wanted a pony when I was a girl," Mom said. "I used to enter dozens of contests with hopes of winning a pony of my own. It's a good thing I didn't win," she finished cheerfully as they pulled into the driveway. "We lived in Torrance, California. There was nowhere to keep a pony. Besides, if I had gotten involved with horses, I probably would not have met and married Dad, and then I would not have had you." Mom parked the car and gazed at Jenny. "And I wouldn't trade you for anything."

Dad pulled in right after them, parking his big red work truck next to the station wagon. Jenny and Mom hurried out to greet him.

"How are my girls?" he asked, kissing them both.

"Just fine, Dad. Did you know that Mom always wanted a pony when she was a little girl, and she used to enter all these contests to win one, but she never did?" Jenny jumbled all the words together in her haste to get them out. Dad's eyebrows flew up in surprise.

"No, Jenny, I didn't know that." He threw a mischievous glance at Mom, then exclaimed, "Well, at least we know whose side Jen gets it from, and thank goodness it's not mine!"

Thursday and Friday went by so quickly that Jenny felt as though she must be in another dimension. It was unbelievable that camp was over and life was going to have to return to normal.

After lunch on Friday, Jenny sat under the crabapple tree with eyes closed. She drew a long breath through her nose, inhaling the barnyard perfume. She could smell horse sweat and leather tinged with the lemony scent of the fly spray they sprayed on the horses.

She sat there for a long while, thinking and praying quietly. "Father, thank You for sending me to this place. I don't know how I can return to life without horses, but I trust You. I want You to come into my life and make it completely Yours. I want You to be more important to me than even the horses. I commit my life to You, Lord Jesus. Please come into my heart and make it Your own. I know You will give me the strength to live without horses. Amen."

Jenny opened her eyes and looked around her. Nothing had changed, but she felt peaceful. She spent the rest of her last afternoon riding and cheerfully helping the other girls whenever she was asked.

Mom arrived just after five o'clock and walked up to meet Jenny. She put her arm around Jenny's shoulder and squeezed gently. "How are you holding up, gorgeous?" she asked.

"I'm fine, Mom. I had a talk with God today, and everything is just fine."

They found Kathy to say their goodbyes. Kathy shook Mrs. Thomas's hand and thanked her. Then she turned back to the other girls to speak to them. Jen and Mom walked to the car together and climbed in. They were beginning to back up when Kathy knocked sharply on the window. Mom jumped, then snapped her head forward. She quickly rolled the window down. "Yes, Kathy, did you need something?" she asked.

"I'm sorry I scared you, Mrs. Thomas," Kathy apologized. "I need to speak to you and your husband privately. May I call you?"

Mom looked a little startled but remained gracious. "Of course, please call us tonight," she agreed. Jenny turned to wave at Kathy and their eyes met. Kathy gave her another mysterious wink. *Well, at least I'm not in trouble,* she thought as they drove away.

"That's odd," exclaimed Mom. "Why would she need to speak to me and your father? Did you do something that I should know about, Jenny?"

Jenny shook her head.

❧ ❧ ❧

At eight o'clock the phone rang. Mom answered it, and Jenny watched her face intently. Mom covered the mouthpiece with her hand, talking to Dad.

"Mike, it's Kathy. She wants you to pick up the extension." Dad walked into the kitchen, while Jenny sat on the sofa trying to read her mother's face. Mom turned around, speaking softly.

What on earth is going on? thought Jenny. *Everyone is acting too weird.* Finally Jenny heard Mom say, "We need to talk about this. Can we let you know tomorrow? Fine. Thank you for calling. Goodbye." Click.

Dad wandered back into the room, and Mom turned around with a faraway look in her eyes. They sat down on the couch with Jenny and Dad began.

"Jenny, Kathy said that you have more natural talent than anyone she has ever seen, and that you were a big help to her this week. She wants to know if you would like to work for her for the rest of the summer. She would like you to assist her with teaching and barn work. In exchange you will be able to take a lesson a day on Chance, plus she will *pay* you to muck out stalls. Would you like to do that?"

"Would I? Would I? When can I start?"! Jenny shrieked joyfully, jumping up and down.

Mom and Dad sat on the sofa squeezing each other's hands, grinning with delight.

Chapter Eight

"I am so excited to have some help mucking today," Kathy said pleasantly, after Jenny's mom dropped her off for her first day of work.

"I'm excited just to be here," said Jen eagerly. "Tell me what to do. I'm gonna be the best stablehand you ever had."

Kathy grinned, batting away the gnats, "I know you will, especially since you're the *first* stablehand I've ever had. I asked you because of your attitude and your talent. This is *hard* work anytime, but in the summer, when it is so hot . . . ooo-wee, you need to be careful! I don't want you passing out on me. We're not looking for a world record in barn mucking. OK?" Jenny nodded with a big smile.

Jenny started with Chance's stall. She led him out of his stall, into the empty stall at the end of the row. She flipped on the big box fan in that stall and checked the water bucket. *Full.* Then she pushed the empty wheelbarrow to the door of Chance's stall and began sifting through the sawdust. The gnats were relentless and they kept diving into her eyes and nose.

"Here," Kathy called from behind her, "Turn the fan on in that stall while you're mucking."

The difference was amazing. She was cool and bug free. *Now I see why they each have a fan,* she thought, looking down the row of stalls.

Jen had mucked three stalls when hunger overcame her. *Peanut butter and jelly. Yuck.* She could only imagine what her sandwich looked like now. A cowbell clanged from down at the farm house.

"Lunch time," Kathy called from Ebony's stall. "Now that you're one of the employees, you can come in to eat with us."

The girls walked down the hill to the yellow farmhouse. The screen door slammed behind them as they entered the kitchen. Cool air embraced Jen's body. She let out an involuntary sigh. "Aahhhh." All of Sonrise Farm stopped for lunch. The kitchen was huge, and in the center of it stood a gnarled oak table that easily sat twelve. Large, sunburned men began filing in and sitting.

Jenny tried, in vain, not to stare. *Who are these men?* she wondered. *I've never even seen them.*

"Everyone, I would like you to meet my assistant," announced Kathy loudly over the growing noise. "This is Jenny Thomas, she is going to help me with camp for the rest of the summer."

Kathy nodded to the tall, dark-haired man seated at the head of the table. "This is my dad, Mr. O'Riley."

The man smiled broadly at Jenny, his eyes twinkling. He leaned across the table to engulf her hand. "So happy to meet you, little Jenny" he boomed, in a thick Irish brogue, shaking her hand vigorously. "My Kathy has told me about you. Welcome to Sonrise Farm."

"And this," continued Kathy, "is my mom, Mrs. O'Riley, but you can call her Mrs. O if you want. Everyone else does."

Kathy's mother, a plump woman with rosy cheeks and big

blue eyes, smiled at Jenny as she placed a brimming bowl of stew with chunks of tender carrots and potatoes. After Mrs. O had served everyone including herself, Mr. O'Riley said the blessing.

"Heavenly Father, we thank You for this food, we thank You for the hands that prepared it. We ask that it nourish our bodies as You would nourish our souls. Thank You also for Jenny, our newest helper. Keep us all safe and happy today. Amen."

"Amen," chorused the table.

Jenny looked around at the folks eating with her. Jenny, Kathy, and Mrs. O'Riley were the only females. They laughed, joked, elbowed each other and had a wonderful time. They were like a big, happy family.

"Kathy, who were all those guys?" Jen inquired after lunch.

"Those are the men my dad hires to help when it's hay time. We're doing the first cutting this week."

Jenny looked around. There were fields all around them. For miles it seemed. *I never thought of Sonrise Farm beyond the camp,* she realized.

Kathy chuckled at Jen's expression. "Come on, I'll show you around the whole farm and tell you what we *really* do here." They saddled up Chance and Poppet.

Poppet was Kathy's mare, and was she gorgeous. Her glossy coat was creamy white, and she had a luxurious floor-length tail. Her dainty intelligent face held huge dark eyes that looked almost Arabian. Her long neck was gracefully set on a perfect shoulder.

"She is the most beautiful horse I've ever seen," Jenny whispered. Kathy smiled as she rubbed Poppet's neck.

Kathy and Jenny rode through the ten-acre pasture where the school horses lived. Kathy hopped down to open a big metal gate. She closed it after Jen and Chance went through. Then they went through another gate and over a small hill. As they

reached the top of the hill, Jenny could see acres and acres of pasture.

"Sonrise Farm has 320 acres," Kathy began. My parents bought this land years ago when they emigrated from Ireland. We grow our own hay, cut it, and bale it for the winter. Over there is our broodmare barn where the foals are born. My father breeds jumpers. Most of the mares in that barn are Irish Thoroughbreds. Dad and I will be breaking the two-year-olds later this summer. We usually sell the ones that won't make the big time. My dad's dream in life is to breed a Grand Prix jumper. So far we haven't come upon the right combination of genes. But it is just a matter of time."

Breathe . . . breathe. Am I dreaming? No. Here she was, sitting on a horse on a hill, talking about breeding jumpers. She remembered her first day at Sonrise Farm and the seemingly misspelled sign. *Mom was right, this had to be an answer to prayer.*

"Thank You, Father," she whispered staring at the green fields around her.

Kathy glanced back at her. "I'm sorry, I couldn't hear you. What did you say?"

"Oh . . . um, I was just thanking God for allowing me to, well, to be here in this fantastic place," Jenny replied, feeling foolish.

"Ah," nodded Kathy, "I do that all the time."

Kathy and Jenny rode all over Sonrise Farm looking at the foals, the yearlings and the young horses already being ridden. Kathy explained the conformation defects in some of the youngsters, while Jenny listened intently.

Finally, the two of them went into the broodmare barn. Most of the foals had been born in March or April and were going through that leggy, gangly stage. It was amazing to imagine these delicate creatures growing up to be the large, powerful animals they were destined to be.

The girls put their horses into empty stalls and went to see each baby. The last foal on the left was a coal black colt with white stockings on his front legs, and a long, white blaze on his face. He was absolutely stunning.

Kathy stood beside her and said, "Every time I see a foal I am reminded of how awesome our Creator is. Look at these perfect babies, their tiny hooves and sweet little manes. He is a mighty God."

"Amen," echoed Jenny.

The girls smiled at each other. "It seems we have more than horses in common," Kathy observed. "Agh," she yelped, tapping her wrist watch, "We've gotta go; your mom is going to be here in fifteen minutes, and we still need to feed the school ponies. Quick, let's hop on and trot back to the school barn." They trotted the whole way back, and Jenny really felt like she was getting the hang of posting.

At the barn Jenny followed Kathy, watching closely as she dished up the grain for the different horses. Some got pellets, some oats, some oats and corn.

"Kathy," Jenny exclaimed, "there must be six different feeds in here, and you know who gets what. How do you remember it all?"

Kathy smiled, "You get used to it, and soon you too will be doing this by heart."

Jenny shook her head doubtfully. They were about half-way through with the feeding when Mrs. Thomas arrived. "Can I help?" she asked, ducking through the railing.

"Sure, Mrs. Thomas, come on over," Kathy called back.

The three of them finished feeding, then turned the horses out into the pasture for the evening. "Why are you putting the horses out at night?" asked Mrs. Thomas. It did seem strange to have them in during the day, then out at night.

"All of our horses are in during the day and out at night

during the summer months," explained Kathy. "Otherwise they get sunburned and eaten alive by flies."

Jenny could attest to the eaten by flies part. Some of the horse flies she had seen should have a pilot's license.

Mom drove home while Jenny chattered a mile a minute about the foals and what Kathy had said about God's handiwork.

"I'm not surprised that someone who lives at a place called Sonrise Farm would say that," smiled Mom.

The summer days slipped by like a warm breeze. Jenny relished every waking moment. Her riding skills grew daily, and she developed an insatiable appetite for learning. She read every horse book she could find and continued her daily lessons with Kathy. By August, the girl who had never had a lesson before June began to jump. She loved the sensation of flying over even a tiny cross rail. Her position and balance were perfect.

"I've never seen anyone take to horseback riding so quickly," Kathy exclaimed one day. "How do you do that?"

"How do I do what?" Jenny asked.

"How do you keep your leg so still and correct when you are jumping? I've been riding for eighteen years, and I still have trouble with my leg position."

"I don't know," Jenny answered, feeling a rush of pleasure from the compliment.

Jenny's arms and back grew strong from the shoveling and riding and her eye for good horses grew strong as well. She knew what good conformation was, and she knew what a good jumper should look like. Jenny could almost feel her skills growing, and better yet, she could sense Kathy's growing confidence in her.

One day the girls went to the training barn where the young jumpers lived. Kathy allowed Jenny to watch as she worked with a four-year-old. This horse was a handsome seventeen hand dark bay gelding named Magnum Force. His large, intelligent eyes followed Kathy as she walked around him.

Jenny could see that Kathy was brushing the young gelding gently. The young horse stood impatiently, swishing his tail and stamping his feet. Kathy finished quickly and sprayed the youngster with fly spray. "Shh, Magnum . . . it's OK. You have to be really patient with these little guys, and remember that they have sensitive skin," she added as she mounted.

Jenny walked beside Magnum, looking way up at Kathy. *There is nothing little about this guy,* she thought. Jenny escorted Magnum and Kathy to the training ring, closed the black metal gate, then perched on the top rail of the ring. Once in the ring, Kathy called Jenny over. "Would you like to get on Magnum and have a lesson?"

"Would I?"! exclaimed Jenny. "*You know it!*" She could barely wait for Kathy to dismount. She put her foot in the stirrup and swung gracefully onto the tall, young horse. Magnum moved around, turning his head to see who was on his back. Jenny leaned forward, patting him on the neck. "It's all right, Magnum, we are going to be good friends," she crooned. Jenny felt him relax under her, and she gave him a little squeeze with her legs. They began walking around the ring.

After twenty minutes Jenny looked around for Kathy and, with horror, found her sitting ringside. She brought Magnum around, stammering her apology. "I . . . I . . . am so sorry," she began. "I started riding and totally forgot you were here. It was really rude of me and . . ." Kathy cut her off in mid sentence.

"Jenny, it's all right. I conducted a little experiment, and I'm happy to say that you passed with flying colors." Kathy did not offer any other information, and Jenny didn't ask. It was rather mysterious.

The next day Jenny and her folks went to church as usual. The sermon was about Proverbs 37. Jenny pricked up her ears and sat up a little straighter. Pastor Jeff was saying what her dad had said weeks ago! She listened carefully, snuggling a little closer to her father.

"Jesus wants us to have a deep understanding of who He is," the pastor said. "He wants us to have heart knowledge, not just head knowledge."

That's it, she thought. *I had head knowledge, but now He is in my heart.* After the sermon, the congregation bowed their heads to pray. Jenny thought about Proverbs 37 and decided to dedicate her riding to God. *Father, I want to always put You first in my life,* she prayed. *I want You to be glorified through my riding, for as long as I am able to continue. I don't know what the future will hold, but I dedicate everything I do and everything I am to You.*

Jenny's soul filled with peace. She didn't know what was going to happen to riding once school started again, but she was thankful that a loving God was in charge of her life.

Later that weekend, Jenny took her parents by Sonrise Farm. She wanted them to see Magnum. The trio was walking towards the training barn when they heard a beautiful clear voice singing "Amazing Grace."

As they approached, Jen realized the songbird was Kathy. She was mucking out stalls and singing praise songs at the top of her lungs. She stopped abruptly when she heard them approach. "Hi! You guys surprised me." Her face was pink from exertion or embarrassment.

"I wanted to introduce my parents to Magnum Force," Jenny explained.

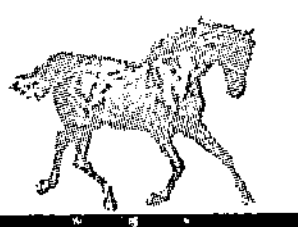

"Oh," Kathy said, regaining her composure. "Go ahead, Jen. You know where he is." Kathy touched Mrs. Thomas's sleeve as Jenny ran on ahead. Magnum stood sleeping in his stall. Jen's voice startled him. She rubbed his face and whispered to him. His eyes grew sleepy as he relaxed again.

Jenny looked back down the aisle to see where everyone had gone and saw her folks standing with Kathy, deep in conversation. Jenny cocked her head, straining to hear. The acoustics in the barn only allowed her to catch snippets of sentences.

Kathy's voice: "Jenny's . . . talent . . . ability. Young horses . . . help train . . . hard worker."

Dad's voice: "I'm worried . . . safety . . . what about . . ."

Jenny tried to ignore the discussion and continued stroking Magnum. "Well, Magnum, it sounds like they are deciding our future down there," Jenny whispered, placing her face against the gelding's soft nose. Her eyes closed as she enjoyed the tickling of his long whiskers on her freckled cheek. When Jenny opened her eyes, her folks were walking towards her, hand in hand.

"Here, Mom, give him a carrot," Jenny instructed. "Break it into pieces and hold your hand out flat."

"Ooo, it tickles," Mom giggled, feeling Magnum's whiskers brush her hand."Boy, Jenny, he is really big!" Dad stated, sounding impressed. The three of them spent about an hour at the barn. Jenny and Kathy gave them the grand tour of the camp, including the big yellow farmhouse where they met the rest of the O'Rileys.

The car ride home was filled with cheerful chatter from the back seat as Jenny described each horse in the jumper barn. She knew all of them by name. She was able to describe why some of them had jumper potential and why some didn't. Only time would tell if she were correct in her assessment.

Once home, Mom and Dad disappeared into their room for several minutes. Jenny changed out of her church clothes and wandered into the kitchen.

"Mom, Dad, where are you?" she called.

"Coming, we'll be there in a minute," Mom answered.

Weird, thought Jenny. Her stomach complained loudly. *Oh well, I guess I will start making lunch.* She pulled out some left-overs from last night's dinner and began to warm them in the oven. She picked a ripe tomato from the garden and pulled some crispy iceberg lettuce out of the fridge. By the time her parents came in from changing their clothes, Jenny was putting potato chips on the plates and setting them on the table.

"Jenny, that looks wonderful! Thank you so much!" exclaimed Mom. They all sat down at the table and bowed their heads to say grace.

"Heavenly Father," prayed Dad, "we thank You for this food that You have provided for us. We thank You for supplying everything we need. We also thank You for the opportunity that has been presented to Jenny today. We ask for Your blessing upon her and her continued safety. Amen."

"Amen," echoed Jenny and her mom in unison.

Jenny looked at her father, puzzled, her long fingers playing with a potato chip. "What opportunity are you talking about, Dad?" she asked.

"Today while we were at Sonrise Farm, Kathy asked us if you could stay on there as a working student. She'd like you to help her train the young horses. She will pay you, and she'd like you to continue to ride once school starts. Your mom and I needed to pray about it, and we have decided that it is all right with us. There *are* some conditions. Once school starts, your grades must stay the same or better, and you must put 10 percent of your money into a savings account, and 10 percent into the offering plate at church. With those conditions in mind,

you may decide for yourself whether you would like to take this job."

Would she like to take this job? *Of course. It's a dream job!* She leaped up and did her now customary war whoop and dance around the kitchen table. When she flopped back down in her chair panting, her face was red from excitement and exertion. She grinned at her parents and they grinned back.

After lunch Dad phoned Kathy, "Kathy? Jenny is thrilled by your offer. We have prayed about it. There are a few conditions you should know about." Dad explained the conditions to Kathy and told her that if Jenny failed to meet them, he would have to end the arrangement.

"Sounds fair to me," said Kathy. "We'll start tomorrow."

Jenny woke with the dawn. She slid out of bed and peered through the blinds. The rising sun peeked over the faraway trees. It looked like a huge, fiery globe. Jenny was transfixed even as she tried to look away. She threw open the shades and curled up in her beanbag chair. She allowed the majesty of the sunrise to fill her with awe for a God who could create such radiance. He was *her* God, and He created this miracle every morning.

"Father God," she whispered, "thank You for letting me share this moment with You. You are an awesome God. I want my life to be a witness to You." She pulled out her Bible and read Psalm 37 verses 5 and 6, again and again.

" 'Commit your way to the Lord; trust in him and he will do this: He will make your righteousness shine like the dawn.' " *Wow,* she thought, feeling the warmth of the sun on her face. *He will make my righteousness shine like the dawn. I wonder what that means?* The little house began to stir. Dad was up and in the shower. Jenny heard her mother's slippers swishing down the hall.

"Mom," she called quietly. Mom opened the door and peered into Jenny's room. Her eyes clamped shut by the intensity of sunlight.

"Whoa, it's bright in here, Jenny!" exclaimed Mom. "Why are you up so early?"

"I've been spending time with God," Jenny explained. Mom sank into the beanbag chair with Jenny. She tenderly pulled a stray lock of hair out of Jenny's face and tucked it behind her ear.

"Mom, what is righteousness?"

Mom looked surprised. "Righteousness means right with God," she explained.

The two of them sat shoulder to shoulder in the squishy beanbag chair watching the beautiful dawn. Mom broke the reverie. She struggled out of the beanbag chair and helped Jenny up. "That thing is like quicksand," she complained.

"I know," Jenny smiled. "That's why I like it. It is so comfy."

Mom started into the kitchen to begin breakfast.

Jenny waited to start her shower until she heard Dad stop the water from his. The water pressure in the old house just couldn't handle two showers at once. She lathered her hair with shampoo and pulled the long locks forward. She had been out in the sun all summer and her hair had bleached out to platinum. Then she dressed quickly and joined her parents in the kitchen. She loved these early mornings together, eating breakfast and gabbing about the day. Sometimes it was the only time she saw her parents together until dinner.

The day usually went something like this: First Jenny fed the school horses and the jumpers. She loved the soft whickering and "come hither" expressions on *some* of their faces. Others pinned their ears and did mini bucks in place. Jenny quickly dumped grain into each feed tub, checked the water bucket, and went on to the next one.

It was fascinating to watch the different horses eat their grain. Some of them drove their muzzles into the tub. Some gently gathered a mouthful while looking around peacefully.

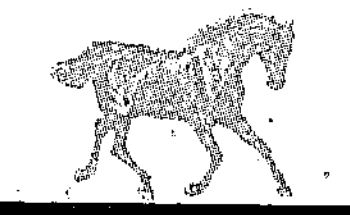

Others swished their tails angrily, kicking imaginary enemies while they ate.

Magnum was a quiet eater. He dipped his velvety nose into his bucket and took a mouthful. Then he would gaze around him, dropping half of his food into the shavings. It took him twice as long as anyone else to eat.

After breakfast, Jenny took each horse out of his stall and tied him in the crossties. She groomed him carefully, then picked out each hoof with a hoofpick. She finished every grooming with the mandatory fly spray.

Sometimes she sprayed her own arms. The flies were ruthless; and some were so large, you couldn't kill them with your bare hand. They definitely preferred Jen's hairless flesh to the horsehide, so she was constantly fending them off.

After Jenny groomed and sprayed each horse, she took the wheelbarrow into the stall to do a quick muck out. She was learning which horses were safe to work around and which ones weren't. She noticed that Kathy only allowed her to ride the "safe" ones.

Following chores, Jenny began riding. She liked to start with Magnum because he was her favorite. Kathy met her in the training ring to demonstrate some stretching exercises. The training ring was much smaller than the schooling ring because it was easier to control a young horse when he couldn't get too much speed. A horse would have a hard time going faster than a canter in the training ring.

Jenny put Magnum through his paces, and they worked on downward and upward transitions. She asked him to halt, walk, trot, and then walk and halt again. These exercises were tedious, but Jenny knew this was the best way for Magnum to build muscle and balance. She was infinitely careful with the horse's soft mouth, and she tried to use her back and legs to turn and stop him.

It was an amazing process. Jenny had always thought that you turned and stopped a horse by pulling on the reins, but it was much more complicated than that. She had to use her entire body to tell him what to do with his body.

After Magnum, Jenny usually rode a lovely bay filly named Sara. Sara was a sweet, but nervous mare. Jenny patiently used her legs and back until Sara relaxed and responded.

"You are doing great!" yelled Kathy from across the ring. "I can really see improvement in her concentration."

Jenny looked down at Sara's neck; she too could see the soft bend in the muscles. The young mare's ears flicked back as she listened to Jenny's voice. Both horses were almost ready to start jumping. Jenny leaned forward and gave the filly a gentle pat on the neck. Sara relaxed her jaw, chewing on the bit.

The three of them walked back and Kathy turned off at the school barn where Poppet lived. "I'll meet you back here in twenty minutes. I need to brush Poppet real quick."

"Okey dokey," Jenny agreed, continuing on to the jumper barn. Once there, she slid off Sara and led her to the crossties. She slipped the bridle off and slid the halter on the mare's head then clipped the buckles of the crossties onto each side of the halter so that the horse was tied from both sides. Then Jenny unbuckled the girth and took the saddle off Sara's back. There was a square sweat mark where the saddle pad had been. Sara heaved a large sigh as her eyelids began to droop.

"Feeling sleepy, little girl?" murmured Jenny. She gave the mare a carrot as she poured some liniment into a bucket of water. She nabbed a big sponge and plunged it into the bucket. The liniment stung as it made contact with her work-chapped hands.

Jenny sponged Sara off, paying special attention to the

sweat marks. She used the sweat scraper to scrape off the excess water, then deftly unclipped the crossties. Jenny led the mare into her stall, checked the water bucket and walked out. She closed the stall door behind and flicked on the fan.

Sara sighed again, then stuck her big face right in the path of the large box fan. Jenny giggled at the sight and jogged out to meet Kathy for lunch.

After lunch, Kathy and Jenny sat under the gnarled crabapple tree. The spot had a great view of the school horse barn, and you could see a corner of the jumper barn where Magnum and the other four-year-olds lived. Together the girls talked about plans for the school and the jumpers.

Jenny realized that Kathy's first love was teaching. The jumpers were really Mr. O'Riley's passion. Kathy wanted to help her father as much as she could and she did know so much about training these animals.

Kathy said, "Jenny, after the last cutting of hay is finished, my dad will be in the jumper barn constantly. I know it seems like he doesn't care right now but it's only because he is too busy. He will be driving us crazy. Actually, he'll be driving *me* crazy. You will be at school. We have what? Four more weeks, then you'll abandon me. I want to tell you, I know I don't say it much, but I'm so thankful to have found you. You cannot know what a big help you have been to me this summer. I have been truly blessed by your company."

Tears rushed to Jenny's eyes. Kathy felt blessed by her presence? Jenny was speechless for a moment, but she took a deep breath and looked at Kathy. Kathy's eyes were teary too! Wow.

"Kathy," began Jenny. "I cannot even begin to tell you what this summer has meant to me. I have been doing things I never thought I would be able to do. I have been learning stuff from you, and from the horses. It has been the most amazing summer I've ever had."

She wanted to go on and say something very meaningful, but she couldn't think of a thing. Kathy didn't seem to mind at all, and the girls sat silently for a few moments, enjoying the shade and the companionship.

After five minutes or so, Kathy stood up and gave Jenny her hand. "Oof, you are getting heavy," complained Kathy. "What have you been eating?"

"Spaghetti, of course," giggled Jenny. She released Kathy's hand and Kathy stumbled backwards.

"Aaaiieeee!" Kathy screamed in mock terror. "See if I ever help you again, you ungrateful child."

Laughing, the girls made their way to the jumper barn to feed lunch to the horses. Every horse looked alert and hungry. Every horse except Magnum. Jenny walked quickly to his stall and peered in. The big horse had pawed all of his bedding into a pile in the center of his stall. His mane and tail were littered with shavings. His dark brown coat was black with sweat. He did not notice Jenny standing there. Suddenly, he groaned and went down again.

Kathy appeared instantly. "We have to get him up. He can't roll. Hurry. Give me his halter." Barking orders like a drill sergeant, she entered Magnum's stall and attempted to put the halter on his head, but his legs were flailing dangerously. "Give me that dressage whip!" she commanded. Jenny looked around wildly, then saw the long black whip in the corner. She managed to hand it to Kathy through the slats of the stall door.

Kathy backed herself into the corner of the stall, shouting at Magnum to get up. She raised the whip and struck him again and again. Finally, the shouting and whipping penetrated the

fog of pain, and Magnum stumbled to his feet. Kathy snapped the halter on quickly, yelling, "Jenny! Go get my dad. He's still in the house. Call the vet while you're there. My mom knows the number. Go . . . GO!"

Jenny bolted. She burst through the screen door, shouting for Mr. O'Riley. "Magnum!" she panted.

He jumped up and charged out the door. Jenny's eyes followed him as he raced toward the jumper barn. She needed to do something else. What was it? What did she need to do? Oh. The vet. She had to call the vet.

"Mrs. O'Riley . . . call the vet . . . something is wrong . . . with Magnum." Jenny could hardly get the words out. Her breath came in ragged gasps. She had never seen anything like Magnum's eyes, staring in stark terror.

Mrs. O'Riley handed the phone to Jenny. "Jenny, you tell the vet what you saw, so he will know what to bring."

Jenny grabbed the phone and held it to her ear. It rang and rang and rang again. *What if he isn't there? What do we do then? Is Magnum going to die? Oh, Father, please don't let him die.*

A feminine voice answered the phone. "Dr. Davis's office, may I help you?"

"YES . . . yes . . . my name is Jenny Thomas, I work at Sonrise Farm and Magnum Force, one of the four-year-olds, is very sick!"

"What seems to be the problem?" asked the receptionist calmly.

"I don't know, but he is sweaty and rolling around in his stall," Jenny panted.

"Ah, sounds like colic. I will radio Dr. Davis now. He should be there within fifteen minutes. Call me back if things get dramatically better or worse."

Jenny hung up the phone and flew from the kitchen, banging the screen door behind her. Down at the stable, Mr. O'Riley had a syringe and a vial in his hand. He drew up 20 c.c.'s of a clear liquid and stuck the covered needle in his mouth. He grasped the needle cover with his teeth, pulling it off. He spat the cover onto the ground and slapped Magnum's hindquarters. He plunged the needle into the spot where he had slapped. Then he pushed the contents of the syringe into the large gluteus muscle.

"Now let's walk him," he said. "Kathy, see if he will go with you." Kathy tugged on the lead rope but Magnum just stood, head straight up and trembling. His eyes rolled wildly, and Jenny heard his teeth grinding.

Mr. O'Riley grabbed the whip and smacked him—hard. Magnum leapt forward and Kathy took up the slack. They managed a few steps before the horse pulled up. His knees began to buckle. Mr. O'Riley whacked him again, and they trotted a few steps more. Kathy and her father yelled at him to "walk on," while Jenny caught her breath.

Soon the three people were yelling and slapping the horse every time he tried to stop. Magnum finally submitted to the walking and Jenny followed right behind him with the whip. The strange foursome had managed to stumble around the yard twice when a blue pickup screeched into the driveway.

A wiry white-haired man jumped from the cab and strode energetically up the incline from the driveway. "What's the problem here?" boomed Dr. Davis in his Texas twang. In spite of the calamity, the vet was calm and smiling.

Jenny felt a flicker of hope. *Maybe it's not so bad,* she thought.

Mr. O'Riley ran to meet him. "Well, Doc, this is Magnum, one of my most promising four-year-olds. He is colicking . . . badly. I gave him 20 c.c.'s of painkiller in the muscle about fifteen minutes ago. He seems a little better but still determined to roll." Mr. O'Riley removed his baseball cap, and ran his fingers nervously through his hair. "I can't afford to lose this one," he said.

"Well, we will give it our best, won't we, girls?" Dr. Davis smiled and winked at Jenny.

How can he be so light hearted? she wondered.

The vet brought another vial of medication from his bag and drew up 10 c.c.'s of the liquid.

"What is that?" Jenny whispered to Kathy.

"It's probably a heavy tranquilizer," replied Kathy. Dr. Davis heard Kathy's answer.

"Yer right, Miss Kathy, this syringe holds enough sedative to put you or me out for a couple of days. What this will do is relax this young horse so his intestines and bowels can unkink themselves. Did you know Miss . . . what is your name?"

"Uh, Jenny Thomas."

Dr. Davis talked while he worked. "Did you know Miss Thomas, that horses put out almost eighty pounds of manure a day? If that production is shut down, they can get in real trouble very quickly, as you probably saw today. Horses live on fiber and water and their bowels move about once every hour. We are hoping to reverse Magnum's blockage by stopping the pain. Hopefully, everything will pass through on its own. If it does *not* pass, then we will have to re-evaluate. Some horses require surgery to remove a blockage. We will just wait and hope for the best."

The vet turned to Mr. O'Riley, "Let's put him in a stall and I'll give him some mineral oil. Then we can let him rest for a while. He won't roll with all these drugs in his system." Kathy and Jenny led Magnum back to his stall. The drug had already taken effect and he swayed drunkenly as he walked. He stumbled on the step into his stall, then stood looking miserable.

Dr. Davis carefully poked a long flexible tube into Magnum's left nostril and kept pushing. About three feet of the tubing disappeared. The vet blew into the end of the tube to be sure he had reached the stomach. Jenny could hear the

gurgling of stomach acid from where she stood. Then the tube went into a bucket full of thick mineral oil. Dr. Davis pumped what looked like bug fumigator and delivered all of the oil into Magnum's stomach. Dr. Davis then pulled the tube gently out of the gelding's nostril. Magnum kept his nose in the far corner, his chin almost in the sawdust. A thin string of drool hung from his mouth. He was a pitiful sight.

"He looks like he's going to throw up," Jen whispered.

"I wish he could," said Kathy. "Horses can't vomit. Whatever goes in can only come out one way." The two stood outside the stall praying silently. Kathy whispered to Jenny, "My dad won't put any of his horses through colic surgery. If Magnum is going to recover, it will have to be here."

The afternoon passed slowly for everyone. Kathy and Jenny did their chores quickly so they could keep a watch on Magnum. Everyone on the farm kept popping in to check on the patient.

Dr. Davis had to continue his rounds but he gave Kathy more sedative in a syringe to administer if needed. He also left his pager number, just in case. Jenny went into the house to phone her parents for permission to stay late. Her mother agreed to come at eight instead of five. "How is the horse?" inquired Mrs. O'Riley.

"Dr. Davis sedated him and now we are waiting to see what happens," Jenny replied glumly. As she trudged to the barn she remembered a verse. It was like someone was speaking it straight to her heart. *"Where two or more are gathered, I will be in the midst of them."*

Jenny looked around slowly, then jogged up to the barn. "Can we pray for Magnum?" she asked shyly. She felt funny, like maybe they thought she was a fanatic or something.

"Certainly," said Mr. O'Riley. "That is an excellent idea. Let's join hands and I will start. Lord Jesus, You have said that when two or three are gathered, You will be with them. We ask that

You would be with us now as we pray for Magnum. He is fighting for his life. We ask that You put Your healing touch on him and cure his pain. If he has a blockage, let it pass on its own."

Kathy prayed, "Father, we ask You to heal Magnum. We don't want to see him in such pain."

Then it was Jenny's turn. She had never prayed in front of other people before. She just hoped she didn't sound too stupid. She took a deep breath. *Here goes,* she thought. "Lord, please help Magnum get better fast. Amen."

"Amen," echoed Kathy and Mr. O'Riley.

They looked in Magnum's stall. He looked the same. Jenny felt disappointed.

Every morning for a week, Jenny rushed in to see Magnum, and every morning he stood in the same corner, head hanging. By Saturday he could no longer stand. He lay rigidly in the center of the stall. Jenny could hear him struggling to breathe from the barn door. His large brown eyes were glazed and hopeless.

Dr. Davis came to see him every day, and every day he shook his head in surprise that the horse was still alive. He pulled out his stethoscope and listened for the rumbling and gurgling of healthy bowels. Every morning he heard ominous silence.

Mr. O'Riley stood at the door of the stall shaking his head. "Is he in pain, Doc?" he asked, staring at Magnum's face.

"I don't *think* so," the vet replied. "But it's just a matter of time before his organs fail. I would not allow him to linger too much longer—if he were mine."

Mr. O'Riley nodded miserably. "Let's give him one more day."

The girls helped Dr. Davis put a stomach tube through the nostril of the large animal. Then he pumped a gallon of mineral oil into Magnum's stomach. "Hopefully, this will lubricate things and make them pass faster," he explained. "It would be

better if we could get him to eat something. Right now he is so empty nothing will move."

"How about a thin bran mash that we can feed him with a turkey baster?" inquired Kathy.

Dr. Davis looked at her, nodding sympathetically. "Well, Kathy, it can't hurt him at this point. Make a mash and add some molasses or syrup to get some sugar into him. Give it slowly, so he doesn't choke. I don't see how you are going to be able to get enough into him to make a difference, but you never know. I have to tell you, I have never seen a horse survive *this* long with an impaction. It's incredible that he is even here. He is obviously a real fighter."

"That's what I'm counting on," called Kathy, running to get a bucket of dry bran. She filled the bucket with warm water and half a bottle of maple syrup. She walked carefully into the barn carrying the sticky liquid bran concoction. Cradling Magnum's head in her lap, she filled the turkey baster with the brown formula and squirted the stuff deep into his throat. The horse opened his eyes, but did not struggle. He swallowed the bran with a loud gulp. Kathy fed him the entire bucket while Dr. Davis watched in disbelief.

"Call me if there is a change," he said. "Otherwise I will see you tomorrow morning."

Jenny and Kathy took turns feeding Magnum all day. By the time Jenny's mom came to pick her up, she was a sticky, sweaty mess. She had fed Magnum three buckets of bran mash and mucked out twelve stalls. No one had ridden since Magnum got sick. Jenny climbed into the front seat of the station wagon and stuck her face in the air conditioning vent. She heaved a heavy, exhausted sigh.

Jenny remembered Sara and the way she had sighed and put her face in the fan after being ridden. Suddenly, Jenny got the giggles. She was even beginning to act like the horses. It felt good to laugh again. She had been so worried about Magnum.

"How is the horse today?" Mom asked.

"Not good," replied Jenny. "He is so weak he can't stand anymore. Mr. O'Riley is thinking about putting him down. Dr. Davis is amazed that he is even alive. He says he has never seen a horse last this long with an impaction."

"Well, Jenny, when we get home, we will pray. All three of us. Your dad and I don't know much about horses, but we do know about praying."

Jenny nodded her head sadly. *It will take a miracle,* she thought.

After dinner the telephone rang. Mom answered with her cheery, "Hello." She covered the mouthpiece with her hand and whispered, "It's Kathy. Should we invite the O'Rileys to join us?"

"Great idea," agreed Dad.

"Sure, Mom," said Jenny.

Mom put the phone back up to her ear. "We are just about to start a prayer session for Magnum. Would you like to join us?"

Jenny didn't hear the answer but figured it must be yes because her mother began pulling together cookies and tea. The O'Riley family arrived within a half-hour.

They prayed in thanksgiving for all the horses and for Jenny. They prayed for protection for Sonrise Farm. Then they began praying for Magnum. Mr. O'Riley lifted him up to the Lord and dedicated him. Finally he asked for wisdom and guidance.

After an hour of prayer the room was charged with power. They could *all* feel it. The two families began singing hymns and praise songs. After two hours, the O'Rileys dragged themselves out the door. Nobody seemed to want the evening to end, but they all had to get up early and Kathy needed to give Magnum his last painkiller shot for the evening.

"This was wonderful. We'll have to get together again soon," Mrs. Thomas said. "Hopefully under happier circumstances."

"Yes, indeed," agreed Mrs. O'Riley. "Thank you so much, it was wonderful!"

"They are dear people," Jenny's mom said as they waved goodbye.

Jenny smiled and nodded, then stumbled to the bathroom and washed her face. She decided to take a quick shower because she felt exhausted. She had just grabbed her pj's and towel when the phone rang. Jenny knew it must be Kathy, so she ran to the living room and grabbed the receiver. She heard her mother on the extension and Kathy on the other end.

"You won't believe it!" Kathy shrieked joyfully. *"I have never been so happy to see manure in my entire life!"*

"What?" asked Jenny's mother.

"So do you think he's all right?" asked Jenny.

"Yes, well . . . he's better. My dad called Dr. Davis out to see him again. Magnum is standing and whickering for some food, and he looks much better to me! Thank You, Lord!"

Jenny felt dazed for a moment, then reality struck. "He is better!" she said out loud. Then she knocked on the door to her parents' room.

"Come in," Mom called.

"Mom, can you believe it?" Jenny's eyes danced as she bounced on the edge of their bed. Mom and Dad looked at each other, smiling.

"Yes, we heard and we believe it," Dad said.

"It is wonderful," Mom agreed. "God is merciful and He hears our prayers."

Jenny hugged her parents, then slipped back to her room feeling humbled and uplifted. She knelt beside her bed like a little child. "Thank You, Lord," she whispered. A tiny tear of joy coursed down her cheeks. Then she climbed under her covers and was immediately asleep.

Jenny was not ready for the teasing sunbeams on her face. She tried to wipe them away with the back of her hand, but to no avail. She surrendered and pulled herself into a sitting position. Then it hit her. *Magnum! Did I just dream it? Is he really OK?*

Rubbing sleep from her eyes, she thought about last night. No, she remembered clearly. God had performed a miracle. They had prayed according to His Word and He had honored that by curing a very sick horse. Suddenly, she couldn't wait to get to Sonrise Farm. "Thank You, Father," she breathed.

Jenny's mom dropped her off at the driveway of the farm and blew her a kiss. Jenny tore up to the jumper barn. Kathy and Mr. O'Riley were there with Dr. Davis in front of Magnum's stall. Magnum was standing, his eyes showing some of the sparkle she remembered. Dr. Davis spoke loudly, obviously excited. "I have never seen a recovery like this before!" he exclaimed. "I don't know what you girls put in that bran mash, but it did the trick."

Kathy and Jenny looked at each other and beamed. "It wasn't the bran mash Dr. Davis," Kathy said softly. "It was the prayer last night. We all met at Jenny's house and prayed for Magnum. When we came home, he was better."

That silenced Dr. Davis. He looked at Mr. O'Riley with a perplexed look.

Mr. O'Riley nodded confirmation of Kathy's statement.

"Well, I don't know what to say," the vet shrugged. "It *is* miraculous that he would suddenly be better after seven days of being impacted. Horses do not survive this kind of thing . . . usually. Whatever you're doing, keep it up."

Dr. Dave walked slowly out to his truck and plunked his bag in the front seat. "Call me if there are any changes," he called back to them. "Otherwise I'll be out in two days to recheck him."

The girls waved goodbye, then rushed back to see Magnum. "Do you think Dr. Davis believed us?" Jen inquired as they gazed at Magnum.

Kathy smiled. "Well, we made him think about it. Let's both pray for him every day and see what happens. Dr. Davis can be our prayer project. Right now we need to take care of this horse project. Magnum is going to need buckets of TLC."

Kathy and Jen brushed every inch of Magnum. The big horse stood quietly and ate it up. He had a few minor sores on his flank from being down so long. Jenny gently applied antibiotic ointment to them. The big horse gently nudged Jen's shoulder. "You're welcome, you big lug," she said to him. "Just get better soon." She patted his wasted shoulder, checked his water bucket, and left the stall.

Kathy had one more session of camp before summer was over. Jenny felt like her right-hand man. They were a team, and Kathy acted as though Jenny had been there forever. This made Jen feel like a real part of Sonrise Farm. Two short months ago she had just been an eager young student. Now she belonged. Maybe it was the close call with Magnum. Jenny just knew that being here was something special, something to be treasured.

She was leaning on her pitchfork, thinking about the past

weeks when Kathy sneaked over and playfully kicked the pitchfork out from under Jenny's chin. "Hey, watch where you're walking!" exclaimed Jenny in mock annoyance. "Can't you see I'm daydreaming here?"

"So sorry, your majesty," Kathy said, bowing with a chuckle. "And what, pray tell, were you dreaming about?"

"I was thinking about this summer, everything that has happened, and wondering about the school year . . . and all that stuff," Jenny replied seriously.

"Oh," said Kathy, suddenly serious too. "Well, school is still a month away and your parents agreed that you could help me during the school year."

"I know," breathed Jenny. "But it will be different. I want to stay here with the horses all the time. What if Magnum colics again, or what if Sara gets sick?"

Kathy laughed. "Jenny, we have managed at this farm for fifteen years. We are very happy to have you here, but we'll survive while you are at school. Just keep your grades up and everything will be fine."

Kathy started to walk away, but stopped mid stride. "*Oh* . . . I remember what I came to talk to you about. This weekend, there is a horse auction at the Hunter's Ridge Equestrian Center. They have one near the end of every summer. I'll be taking Bella and Bud there to sell *and* hopefully picking up some more school horses for next summer. I'd love it if you'd go with me, for company and to ride some of the smaller ponies. Do you think you can go? It's three days away."

"I'll ask my parents: I'm *pretty* sure they'll let me. School doesn't start for a month," Jenny responded.

"Good, it'll be fun. Now get back to work, my pretty . . . hee hee hee," cackled Kathy.

Jenny couldn't help smiling as she finished mucking out her last stall. She thought about Bella and Bud. They wouldn't make it as big time jumpers. She hated to see them sold, but consoled

herself by thinking about them as pleasure horses. They would make fine mounts for someone who wanted a versatile horse.

Later that evening, just after grace, Jenny asked *the* question. "This weekend Kathy is taking two of the four-year-olds to an auction at Hunter's Ridge. She is hoping to buy a couple more school ponies and would like me to try them out for her. May I go?"

Mr. and Mrs. Thomas glanced at each other—relief plainly written on their faces. Dad explained, "We were certain you were going to ask us if you could buy a horse. My business is going well, but I'm not sure that *now* would be the time to get into horse ownership. Your mother and I are very proud of the way you have stuck to your commitment to Kathy and still done your chores at home. Once school starts though, you are going to have a full plate. We think you should try this for a little while before you . . . before we get into the expense of owning a horse."

Jenny nodded silently, astonished. She hadn't even considered owning her own horse. Dad went on. "We'd like to go with you to the auction. It would be a chance for your mom and me to see you in action."

Nodding again, she agreed. "Good, then it's settled," Dad pronounced. He smiled and began eating his dinner. Jenny and her mother rinsed the dishes and loaded them into the dishwasher. Jenny stared at her mom. Mom was pursing her lips like she did when she was mulling something over.

"What's going on here?" Jenny demanded. "You're *both* acting weird tonight."

"Jenny . . . your dad is interested in the horse . . . thing. He thinks that maybe we should buy you a horse. He just wants to figure it out before we commit ourselves. You know how he is. Before we buy a toaster he researches all the different brands and models. It's the way he does things. We don't want to get your hopes up."

"Wow," Jenny said. "I had no idea. I thought you would see the horses as a waste of time and money."

"Well, honey, we have seen the maturity you have gained. We have seen the difference in your spiritual life and—it is a great way to keep you from dating."

"Mom!" Jenny squealed, totally embarrassed. "Who would want to see boys when you can see horses."

"My point exactly," Mom said, smiling. "Seriously though. We have been praying about it and it seems as though God may be saying 'Yes.' But . . . don't go crazy because it will take a while."

Jenny tried not to go crazy with the thought of her own horse but it was difficult. *What kind will I get? A Thoroughbred, of course. What color should it be? A Palomino of course. Should I get a mare or a gelding? Well, a gelding would probably make more sense, but a mare I could breed.*

Yes, I am going nuts, she thought. *A mare so I can breed her. I must be going out of my mind. Oh well, we can all dream about impossible things. Right, Lord?* She fell asleep and dreamed of little Palominos running and jumping.

The day of the auction arrived and Jenny was so nervous she didn't even *try* to eat breakfast. She had never been to an auction before and now she was going as an employee of Sonrise Farm. Jenny caught her folks watching her with amusement as she scurried back and forth getting ready.

The Thomas family met Kathy in the driveway of Sonrise Farm, where Mr. Thomas helped get the two horse trailer hooked up to the truck. "This will make sure I don't go crazy and buy too many horses," Kathy chuckled. "One year I took a four-horse stock trailer. Whew—*that* was a mistake"

They loaded Bella and Bud without a fuss. Jenny climbed into the truck with Kathy while Jen's folks jumped into the station wagon. Jenny kept an eye on the car as it followed Kathy to Hunter's Ridge. They found a shady place to park both vehicles. Kathy hopped out of the truck, and walked briskly to the back of the trailer. "Jenny, come help me with Bella and Bud, will you please?" Kathy called over her shoulder.

Jenny dashed over to help unload the youngsters. The horses backed off the trailer, looking around with huge,

wondering eyes. Kathy handed Jenny Bella's lead rope and they headed toward the main barn to find their assigned stalls. Both horses snorted nervously as they walked. Kathy approached the main barn to look at the roster. "We're in Barn C," she announced looking around. "Stalls 5 and 6. I'm glad they're together—they'll calm each other down."

The girls led the horses into their stalls. Kathy brought in some hay for munching, while Jenny filled water buckets. When the horses were settled, the girls gave them each a carrot and patted them reassuringly on their sweaty necks.

"You two be good," Kathy called as they turned to race back to the trailer, where Jenny's parents waited patiently. The foursome walked into the office of the park and each grabbed a catalog. The flipping pages showed ponies in the front section and horses in the back.

Kathy pulled a pen from her britches pocket. "OK," she said, "here's the deal. The auction is in two parts, first the ponies, then the horses. The first thing we do is read about the animals listed and find the ones that sound interesting. They all have numbers on their rumps and stall doors. We want to see how they act in their stalls. Then we get to ride them. That's where Jenny comes in. Now, if any one gets too wild, you jump right off. No heroics. Got it?"

Jenny saluted crisply, "Yes *sir,*" she said with a giggle.

Kathy found a cute gray Welsh pony and a sweet, but stunted looking, bay Quarter Horse. The bay had a big, stocky body with short pony legs. He was just 14.3 hands—but one inch too big to compete in shows as a pony. "These small horses make great school ponies because nobody else wants them. I doubt if anyone else even bids on this horse," Kathy predicted, stroking the kind face of the bay.

"What exactly is a Quarter Horse?" inquired Mrs. Thomas. "And why do you think you will be the only bidder on this horse? He seems very nice."

Kathy explained. "A Quarter Horse is a breed whose claim to fame is that they are the fastest horse in the world for a quarter mile. You see his large hindquarters? Those are sprinter muscles. This guy is an old timey Quarter Horse. At 14.3 he is technically a horse. Most people want big horses or big ponies. If he were one inch shorter, he would be a large pony, and much more marketable. I know it sounds silly, but folks don't want small horses." It was easy to see that Kathy enjoyed the role of teacher.

Jenny rode both prospects around the ring. The gray pony proved too wild for the school, but the Quarter Horse was as kind as he looked. Jenny rode six other contenders. Some bucked, some tried to bolt, and some attempted to drag her around the ring. She stayed on them all, and once, caught her folks smiling proudly.

By the end of the morning Kathy had three animals marked as school candidates. Now they had to wait for the bidding. They walked into the indoor arena, bought some lunch and claimed a front row seat on the bleachers. They laughed and chatted merrily until the first ponies entered.

The auctioneer began. "Do I hear fiftyfiftyfiftyfifty . . . Fifty!" The auctioneer saluted the opening bidder. "Sixtysixtysixty . . . what do I hear?"

The air became thick with smoke and excitement. Jenny felt every nerve leap to attention as she strained to keep track of the bidding.

A scrubby little buckskin mare went for $150 to a paunchy man in a greasy polo shirt. He patted his sizeable stomach and spat on the ground.

"Who is that man?" Jenny whispered urgently in Kathy's ear.

"Oh, that's the meat man," Kathy said with a grimace. "He'll buy all the cheap ponies and horses. He usually takes them to one more auction, but if he can't double his money, they become dog food. I hate it when he's here because it makes me want to buy them all. I'm sorry he is here today. It makes the auction so depressing."

It certainly is depressing, agreed Jenny. She wanted to keep a close eye on him.

The pony auction ended, and Kathy bought a very nice red roan mare. She dove into the office to fill out her paper work, then rushed back to the bleachers.

"We need to fetch Bella and Bud," she hissed in Jen's ear. Jenny whispered the information to her mother, then jumped up after Kathy. The girls had no trouble leading Bella and Bud back to the indoor arena.

The nicer horses came out first, and there were some beauties. Jenny counted ten Thoroughbreds, including Bella and Bud. The little horse Kathy wanted would be entered near the end of the sale because of his size.

It was still going to be a real trick for Kathy to sell her two and get back in time to bid on the little Quarter Horse. Fortunately, Bella and Bud were the first two horses in the arena. Kathy grinned as Bella sold for $5,000 and Bud sold for $4,200. One family bought them both. Jenny craned her neck around Bella to catch a glimpse. There were two teenage girls clapping their hands in anticipation.

Kathy handed Jen Bud's lead rope and jogged ahead toward the family who had bought the pair. She fished one of her Sonrise Farm business cards from her pocket and handed it to the man. The teenagers took the lead ropes from Jen and led their new mounts away.

"They haven't brought him out yet," whispered Mrs. Thomas as Kathy and Jenny plopped down next to her. Kathy nodded, keeping her eyes glued on the ring. Finally the little bay

stepped out and the auctioneer began. The horse was quiet and calm in spite of all the commotion, looking into the crowd with liquid brown eyes. The meat man began the bidding at $50.

"Oh no you don't," muttered Kathy under her breath. She yelled, "$250!"

The auctioneer tipped his hat at Kathy and the meat man spat on the ground in disgust. There were a few tense moments as Kathy and the meat man went head to head on the bidding. Kathy out bid him and bought her Quarter Horse for $600.00. "A bargain at twice that price," she declared, grinning triumphantly.

Just then a horse entered the arena. The bleachers were nearly empty by this time, but there was an audible gasp from the remaining people. The horse was a tall mare, that looked to be in her late twenties. She was an impossibly filthy rack of bones. Her mane and tail were matted with burs and her whole body was caked with red mud. Jenny could not even distinguish what color she was. She entered slowly, painfully, then stood quietly in the center of the ring, her bony sides heaving. She could not muster the energy to lift her head to see where she was.

Kathy looked at the Thomas's and whispered, "I am *so* sorry you had to see this. These kinds of horses do not usually wind up at *this* sale." Kathy shook her head sadly. "She is the most pathetic thing I have ever seen."

The mare could barely totter around the corner of the ring because she was so lame. Her spine stood up like a sail on her back and her joints looked grotesquely swollen. The horse was obviously near death from starvation. She was the saddest creature Jenny had ever seen. The auctioneer didn't even bother to start a bid. The meat man bought her for $20.00.

Jen and her folks wandered, shaken and disoriented, out

of the dark arena, blinking painfully in the hot afternoon sunshine. Kathy went to collect her new ponies. Jenny could not suppress the overwhelming sorrow she felt. She looked at her mom. Mrs. Thomas stood, biting her lip, trying to hold on to a very large tear that threatened to spill onto her face. Jenny slipped her slender arm around her mom's waist, and they stood together, sharing their grief. The tear slipped and rolled down Mrs. Thomas's face.

Just then Kathy peeked out from around the corner of the trailer. "Mr. Thomas, she chirped, "would you help me load this pony? She is just a *tiny* bit reluctant."

Dad gazed at Jenny and Mom, smiling sympathetically. "I'll just be a moment," he promised. "We'll stop on the way home and grab some early dinner, OK?" Jenny and Mrs. Thomas nodded their heads. *How can he think about food at a time like this?* Jen wondered.

The meat man walked by, leading the emaciated horse. She was having trouble walking on the gravel, but was stumbling along as quickly as she could. The man smacked her with a long, black whip.

The mare turned her face and stared right at Jenny and Mrs. Thomas. Her huge, soft eyes held a mute appeal for help. Jenny searched her mother's horrified face. *We have to do something. What can we do?* She looked around hoping to find an auction official. *Surely this was illegal.*

Suddenly, Mrs. Thomas's look changed to anger. She grabbed Jenny's hand and marched toward the meat man's trailer.

"You stop hitting that horse!" commanded Mrs. Thomas.

The fellow turned his beady eyes on her, looking her up and down, an ugly smile creeping over his face. "I own this animal," he sneered, "bought her fair and square. I can do what I want with her."

Jenny could not believe what happened next. Her sweet,

gentle mother stared the meat man in the eye and declared, "I'll give you fifty dollars for her."

"A hundred," he shot back, looking amazed, "and she's yours."

Jenny frantically grabbed her mom's arm, "I have $100, I'll pay you back!"

Mom squared her shoulders and pulled out her checkbook. She hastily wrote a check for $100 and held it out to the man with a trembling hand. He snatched it like a starving animal. He stepped back and stared at the check, shaking his head in disbelief. His face broke into a grimace of a smile as he shoved the check into his shabby pocket and spat on the ground. He handed the grimy lead rope to Mrs. Thomas, who passed it straight to Jenny.

Chapter Fifteen

Jenny shook her head. It had happened so quickly she could hardly believe it. With the dirty lead rope in her hand, she began to walk slowly toward Kathy's trailer leading the decrepit horse.

As they approached the rig, Kathy poked her head out and nearly fell over. She rushed toward them with Mr. Thomas hot on her heels. "Are you kidding?" Kathy shouted.

Mr. Thomas looked at his wife helplessly and pleaded, "Did you really buy her? Tell me you didn't."

Jenny said quietly, "I am paying Mom back with my money from work."

Kathy snorted. "Jenny, how much did you pay for this filthy rack of bones?"

Jenny lifted her chin and took a deep breath. "One hundred dollars," she declared, "and we would do it again. Right, Mom?"

Mom looked at Dad and shrugged. "Probably, sweets," she answered, sounding unconvinced.

Mr. Thomas patted the creature's ragged neck. The mare gazed at him. "She really does have beautiful eyes," he commented.

Kathy slapped herself on the forehead. "Not you, too. Lis-

ten—you guys don't know anything about horses. You can't go around buying them because they are starving and have nice eyes. You'll go broke!"

Dad wrapped a comforting arm around his wife. She leaned against him and confessed, "I'm sorry, Michael, I don't know what came over me. I watched that awful man beating her and I saw red."

Kathy sighed. "Well, I don't have room in my rig for Methuselah here so I'll run my ponies home and come back for you. OK?"

"OK," chimed the three Thomases. Kathy climbed into her truck just as the mare collapsed to her knees. Kathy leapt back out and ran to where Jenny stood holding the dirty lead rope, stunned. The horse groaned and rolled onto her side.

"Mr. Thomas!" Kathy shouted. "Find the vet! There's one here somewhere."

Mr. Thomas glanced at Jenny and sprinted toward the indoor arena. Moments later Jenny heard the crackly sound of the loudspeaker. "Dr. Davis, will you report to the indoor barn. We have an emergency. Dr. Davis, please report to the indoor ring immediately."

Jenny knelt next to the mare's head. The horse gazed at her, blinking slowly. Jenny held her hand over the mare's eye to block the intense sun. "Hang on old girl," Jenny whispered. "Hang on, Dr. Davis is coming. He'll know what to do."

Jenny heard hasty footsteps behind her. She craned her head around to see the familiar face of Dr. Davis. He said nothing at first, just quickly set to work. "Her heartbeat is slow and weak," he muttered to himself. He pried back her lips and pressed the gum just above her teeth. "Her color is really bad."

Jenny peeked around his shoulder. The mare's gums were grayish white.

Dr. Davis looked around wildly, "We've got to get her out of this sun, she's cooking!" Mr. Thomas and several

male passers-by dragged the mare to the shade of a nearby tree. Jenny grabbed a bucket of cold water and began sponging her. Rivulets of muddy water ran off the mare's hide.

Dr. Davis pulled a long clear I.V. tube from his bag. He attached a long needle to one end and carefully placed the needle into the mare's neck. At the other end of the tube was a plastic bag filled with clear fluid.

"What is that?" Jenny asked breathlessly.

"Lactated Ringers solution," the vet answered. "I can't tell you what exactly is wrong with her, my guess is that her organs are failing. She is in the final stages of starvation. I hope we can prevent her from dying in the parking lot. This is basically sugar water. It may keep her alive long enough for you to get her home."

Jenny didn't hear anything else. She concentrated on the mare's eyes. "Keep looking at me, old girl," she crooned over and over. *Father God,* she prayed silently, *please let her live. I know she's old, but I don't want her to die like this. If I could just keep her for a little while.*

The mare's eyes seemed brighter and more alert. Kathy ran to the truck and pulled out her cell phone. She jogged back. "My dad and three strong men are coming with a stock trailer. We'll fill the trailer with hay and drag her on to it. I think we can do this."

Dr. Davis stood up and rubbed his lower back. "I'll finish up here and meet you at the farm. Whose horse is this anyway?"

Jenny raised her hand. "Mom and I just bought her from the meat man. He was beating her." Her chin shook so hard she could barely talk.

"Oh, I see," said the old vet gently. He reached down and squeezed Jenny's shoulder. "I'll get there as soon as I can," he promised.

Tears trailed down Jen's cheeks when the farmhands from Sonrise Farm arrived and dragged the mare onto a horse blanket. From there they grabbed the corners of the blanket and heaved her up the ramp. Jenny stayed near the horse's head and she and the mare locked eyes. The mare did not even attempt to rise. Mr. O'Riley plucked the needle from the thin neck and wrapped the I.V. tube around the empty bag.

The stock trailer was like a huge stall. Jenny arranged the hay around the emaciated animal. She squatted down so she could gaze into the eyes of the horse again.

"You hang on, do you hear me?" she commanded. The horse rolled her eyes back and groaned. Jenny hopped out of the trailer. "Please be careful, Mr. O'Riley," she pleaded.

"You ride with me Jenny," he answered waving her to him. He smiled kindly at her. "We will go very slow and gentle. You can make sure we do."

After the long agonizing trip, Jenny waited anxiously as they lowered the trailer ramp at Sonrise Farm. *Has she died? Did we make it?* The old horse was still breathing . . . barely. Dr. Davis was waiting. He jogged down from the barn where Magnum lived. The farmhands dragged the horse blanket off the trailer. The horse rolled up onto her chest.

"I don't believe it!" said the vet. "She's looking around." The horse found Jenny's eyes and stared there. Jenny walked backwards up the little hill to the school horse barn, keeping her eyes on the horse. The mare managed to keep her head up to return Jen's gaze.

Kathy ran ahead and led Ebony from her stall. "This converts to a broodmare stall. Let me push the wall back. Then we'll have room."

They pulled the mare into the huge stall where Kathy quickly made a deep bed of straw. Dr. Davis listened to her heart again. "Sounds a little stronger and her color is better.

Let's get her on an I.V. with more Ringer's solution. She's dehydrated and who knows what else."

"I know who knows," whispered Mr. Thomas. Jen craned her neck around to look at him. He winked at her, then bowed his head. Jen sighed and began praying silently too.

"Dr. Davis," Kathy said. "What do you think? Is she too old to try and save? Would it be better to . . . you know . . . end her suffering?"

The vet stood up. "Who said she was old?" he asked, looking confused.

"No one," Kathy replied. "She just *looks* ancient."

"Look at her teeth," said the vet. "She's about six and I'm pretty sure I saw a tattoo on her top lip. She's probably a registered Thoroughbred. This horse has a very strong will to live. It's up to you. I *will* warn you that the chances are very slim that she'll make it, and even slimmer that she'll ever be rideable. She's going to require around-the-clock care for the first week. *You* need to decide this, not me."

Jenny stood and walked to her parents just outside the stall. "I want to try," she pleaded, tears pouring from her eyes. "Please."

Mr. Thomas ran his hand through his hair. "Jen, honey, we don't know that much about horses. How are you going to do this?"

"We'll help," replied Mr. O'Riley.

Mr. Thomas shrugged helplessly. "All right. Give it your best try, Jenny. We'll do whatever we can."

She threw herself into him and squeezed hard. "Thank you, Daddy. Thank you."

Dr. Davis pulled out more bags of liquid. "You'll need these later. Jenny, I'll show you how to change the bags. Just keep her with a steady supply at all times. Let's get that magical

turkey baster you girls used with Magnum and get some food into this poor thing."

Kathy ran to the kitchen while Jenny grabbed some foal pellets from the feed room. They added water and allowed the pellets to become a thin mush. Jenny sat with the mare's head in her lap and squirted a small amount into her mouth. The horse swallowed most of it.

"Excellent," nodded Dr. Davis. "Keep doing that, a couple of basters full every hour. If she gets through the next 48 hours, she'll have a much better chance."

Jenny and Kathy stayed with the mare all night. They took turns napping, watching, and feeding. At sunrise Jen opened her eyes to find the mare staring at her.

"Good morning girl, how are ya'?" Jen crooned.

Kathy stirred and rolled over in her sleeping bag. Jenny prepared the turkey baster for the feeding. The horse raised her head and swallowed the mush easily. Jenny managed to get six basters full into her before the mare laid her big head down, exhausted.

"I know how you feel," Jen whispered, rubbing her own shoulder.

Mr. O'Riley appeared at the stall door. "Let me sit with her for a while," he whispered. "You and Kathy go inside and eat some breakfast. Mrs. O'Riley has cooked up some pancakes and eggs. You need your strength too."

Jenny shook Kathy awake and they stumbled to the kitchen. The fragrance was heavenly. Jen ate a couple of cakes before being overcome with sleepiness. Mrs. O'Riley led her by the shoulders into the guestroom. "You sleep here Jenny. I will call your parents and tell them."

Jen couldn't even answer. She nodded and fell face first, onto the fluffy down comforter.

The big golden horse galloped smoothly through the acres and acres of grass. Jenny raised her arms out like she was flying.

They were *flying. The Palomino mare was so smooth and strong it felt like riding on a warm breeze. They jumped the fence and kept on going . . .*

"Jenny! Jen, wake up. Your horse is thrashing! Get up. We need you." It was Kathy staring intently at Jen's face. "What . . . Oh!" she remembered suddenly. *I have a horse.*

The girls ran to the barn, Jen was fully awake now her heart pounding with fear. What would she find? Mr. O'Riley stood at the open stall door shaking his head. "It doesn't look good girls."

Jenny dived through the open door before anyone could think to stop her. The mare was thrashing about, her eyes wild, nostrils flaring. "Sshhhh, girl," Jenny murmured. "Its all right, I'm here."

The horse quieted immediately. They locked eyes again and the big horse lay back in the straw. Jen took her position near the head so the horse could see her. The mare heaved a sigh and closed her eyes. "Looks like I'm staying put," she said.

Mr. O'Riley shook his head again. "I've never seen anything like that before," he said out loud to himself.

Jenny ate and slept in the big stall with the mare for a week. She longed for a shower but didn't dare risk it. She crept out for longer and longer periods until she could be away for an hour at a time. *What would I do without Kathy?* she wondered as she traipsed to the house for that first shower.

The following week the mare improved so much that Dr. Davis came back to pull the I.V. line out and help them rig up a sling and winch. "It'll do her good to stand up a little," he explained. "You'll need to wrap her legs or she'll stock up."

They wiggled the wide belt under the horse's belly and began the winch. Jenny stood by the mare's head and sang, "Amazing Grace, how sweet the sound . . ."

Kathy pitched in and they sang softly as the mare was pulled slowly into a standing position. They allowed her to stand for fifteen minutes, then removed the wide belt. The horse stood for a moment on her own, then her knees buckled under her. She lay on her stomach and chest and seemed happier. Those fifteen minutes allowed Jen and Kathy to clean the stall and replace the deep bedding around her.

"Do that for twenty minutes tomorrow, then twenty-five minutes the day after and so on," prescribed Dr. Davis. "I do believe we are through the worst of it, Jenny," he smiled.

She grinned back. "Thank you, Dr. Davis, I know you saved her life."

He stared at her solemnly, "I may have been here, but you girls know who really did this. The only reason I even gave you any hope is because I've seen what you two can do or what your God can do."

"He's your God too," Jenny replied.

"Maybe," said the vet doubtfully. "We'll see."

After another week the mare was able to stand by herself, but still couldn't rise without the winch. She had graduated to drinking the mush from a bucket. They fed her small amounts every hour. She drank on her own and whickered when she saw Jenny.

Jenny began trying to groom the still-filthy mare. She began by using the tiny rubber curry comb. The red clay and brambles had so permeated the hair that it required serious pulling and teasing to convince them to release. Jenny worked on small patches at a time so the horse didn't get sore.

What in the world? she wondered, as white strands of mane began to show up in the curry comb. "I thought you were a chestnut," she crooned to the mare. "Now I'm not so sure. Can you wander out here a little and have a bath?"

The mare followed her, stumbling a little but staying up. Jenny didn't have to tie her in place for the bath—the mare just stood in the hot summer sun dozing. Jenny grabbed a bucket and ran warm water from the wash stall. She used the sponge to wet the mare's coat. The horse didn't move. Jen grew bolder. She squirted shampoo into her hand and lathered it into the mare's coat.

Tears sprang up in Jenny's eyes as months of grime came away in her hand. Under all that clay was a golden hide. "You're a Palomino," she breathed, awestruck. "I can't believe it!" She raised her voice. "Kathy! Mr. O'Riley! Come here! You won't believe it!"

They ran from the barn, clearly afraid something terrible had happened. Jen showed them the golden patch. "She's a Palomino," Jen whispered.

Kathy smiled. "I'm calling your folks. They need to see this."

By the time they arrived, Jenny had almost finished bathing the horse. She watched as they talked to Mr. O'Riley all the way up the little hill. They looked up at the same time. Mrs. Thomas drew in a gasp and covered her mouth in shock. Her eyes brimmed with tears, which splashed unnoticed onto her face. She caught Jenny's eye and shook her head. "I . . . I . . . I don't know what to say. It's a miracle. There is no other explanation."

Jenny ran to them and hugged them. "You are right. It's a miracle. I am going to name her Endless Sonrise, Sunny for short. What do you think?"

"Its perfect," her dad said. "Just perfect."

Jenny went home that night for the first time since the auction. Sunny seemed calm and ready to spend her first night alone. Dinner was burgers on the grill. Jenny ate two with all the fixings. "Great burgers, Dad," she mumbled with her mouth full.

"Thanks," he replied. "Would you like another one?"

"No, thanks, I'm stuffed." Jenny popped the last bite into her mouth and leaned back in her seat. She was achy and tired, but she felt fantastic. She had to keep telling herself that this wasn't a dream. She really had a horse, and Sunny really was less than five miles away.

Jenny glanced at her parents; they looked tired too. Swallowing hard to clear the lump in her throat, Jenny said, "Mom and Dad, thank you so much. How can I ever repay you?"

Mom laughed, "Well, you could start by clearing the table and helping me with the dishes."

"Gladly," Jenny answered, taking the plates into the kitchen. That night she fell into bed and snuggled under the covers. She wanted to savor this feeling. She was deliciously sleepy and filled with joy. It was wonderful to be alive. "Father in heaven, thank You for my parents, for Kathy and her folks, and for my beautiful horse. I will dedicate everything I do with her to You. Amen."

Morning arrived much sooner than expected and Jenny tried to ignore it. *Wait! Did I dream that? Do I really own a Palomino?* Suddenly the need to see Sunny was urgent. Her parents were still sleeping so she padded lightly down the hallway into the kitchen, chose some cereal from the pantry and ate slowly as she daydreamed. Mom walked in as she was delivering Sunny's third foal.

"I thought I heard you in here," Mom whispered. "I figured you would be up with the sun." She grabbed a bowl and sat down next to Jen. As she tipped the last of the milk into her spoon, she asked, "Well, do you want to go to the barn now or later?"

"Now, please, Mom," Jenny whined anxiously. "I want to see how Sunny did overnight."

"OK. Just give me five minutes to change and brush my teeth."

The sun was just peeking over the horizon a few minutes later as they turned into Sonrise Farm. It was a glorious sight. Jenny's mom parked the car and they got out quietly so they wouldn't wake anyone in the house. By the time they reached the barn their shoes were squelching with dew. They walked on tiptoe to avoid waking the horses. Jenny's breath stopped as she approached Sunny's stall. She stopped . . . looked in . . . and saw the horse lying on her chest like a huge golden cat. Sunny's chin rested on the ground, her bony sides heaving in and out slowly.

Jenny opened the stall door and slipped inside. As Jenny's mom looked in, Sunny opened her big brown eyes, blinking sleepily. She gave a drowsy nicker and with a huge effort, scrambled to her feet. She shuffled to the open door, searching their hands for treats. Jenny had to laugh at the strong lips that probed the pockets of Jenny's jacket. There was no fooling this horse. She knew right where to look.

Jenny gave her most of the carrots in her pockets and then

looked up at her mom. "Mom, I don't know how to thank you for rescuing Sunny. I know that God has plans for her."

Mom smiled, patting the ragged coat of the mare. "Well sweetheart, I hope that she will be all you want her to be. I would hate to see you disappointed if she doesn't live up to *your* plans."

Jenny stroked Sunny's face. She could see a different Sunny in her mind: fat, round, and happy. She could *see* it. Jenny went to the tack room and pulled out some brushes. She began grooming Sunny's rough coat. The mare leaned into the brush.

Jenny envisioned a different scenario, one where her mother had *not* stepped in. Where would Sunny be if *that* had happened? It was unthinkable. Jenny stopped her frightening thoughts by praying silently: *Father God, thank You for this horse and for my brave mother who had the courage to stand up and save her.* She hugged Sunny's neck for a moment. Then she hugged her mother. "Isn't it amazing, Mom," Jen marveled. "Last month I didn't have a horse, and this morning I have a *Palomino!* I love Sunny so much. I would do anything for her."

"*Why* do you love her, Jen? Has she done anything for you? Would you love her even if you couldn't ride her?"

Jenny answered immediately. "I just love because she's *mine!*"

"Jesus loves us the same way, Jen," her mom said. "*Not* because of our performance. He loves us just because we are His."

Jenny smiled. It was strange but comforting to think about the security of being loved just for being herself.

Jenny gave Sunny one more carrot and came out of the stall. Mom followed, latching the lower part of the Dutch door. The two of them wandered back to the car holding hands.

At home they were surprised to find Dad at the stove cooking scrambled eggs. He grinned sheepishly, looking down at his pajamas and a ridiculously small apron. He bunched the

apron behind his back, and with a flourish, offered them a platter of eggs and toast with the other hand. They accepted, trying not to laugh out loud.

"So, how was the horse?" he inquired, still smiling.

"Wonderful," replied Jenny grabbing some forks from the silverware drawer. "She is going to be wonderful." They held hands and said grace for the breakfast and a Thank You for Sunny.

After breakfast number two, as Jenny changed for church, she noticed her small Bible on the nightstand and picked it up. She sat on the edge of her unmade bed and read Psalm 37, thanking Jesus for the incredible events that had occurred the day before.

Jenny glanced over her shoulder at the poster of the Palomino stallion and was struck by the difference in how it made her feel. It had once been a symbol of all her longing. Now it was just a picture on a wall. Her longing now was to live for Jesus, and to take care of Sunny. *Amazing.* She pulled her blue dress from the closet and got ready for church.

The sermon was about redemption, and Jenny found a parallel between the redeeming love of Jesus and Sunny's redemption. The price had been different. Jenny hadn't died to buy Sunny, but Sunny's fate would have been horrible if someone had not come along to save her. *So,* Jenny thought, *Jesus redeemed me with His blood, and Mom and I redeemed Sunny with a hundred dollars. Sunny and I would both be dead if someone hadn't saved us. Thank You, Jesus for giving your life to save me, and thank you, Mom, for helping me save Sunny.*

When Jenny returned to the barn, Kathy was turning the horses out, and she explained the new regime. It was now cool enough for the horses to be out during the day. As Magnum turned the corner to the pasture, Jenny was surprised by how

well he looked. He was still thin from his almost fatal colic, but he looked fit and ready to start work again.

Jenny mentioned this to Kathy as they mucked out the stalls, and Kathy had to agree. Dr. Davis, the equine vet, was dropping by later. Assuming he agreed, it was decided that they would begin riding Magnum on Monday.

I am mucking out my horse's stall! Would she ever get used to how that sounded? It was awesome! Jenny picked her way around the resting animal. Sunny did not rise, but turned her head and watched, with ears pricked forward, as Jenny walked back and forth, shoveling manure and wet sawdust into the wheelbarrow.

Jenny whistled happily and she could see her mare's ears flick back and forth as Sunny listened to the sweet song of her mistress. Jen scrubbed the buckets and hung them in their places. She filled the water bucket with cool water and laid some fresh hay in the hayrack. One wheelbarrow of clean shavings and it was finished! Jenny looked proudly at the immaculate stall. She did do a good stall.

Next, Jenny fumbled in her pockets for some treats and found some baby carrots. She put them on her flat palm, enjoying the tickle of Sunny's long whiskers on her open hand. Jen grabbed the brushes and began softly brushing the mare's back.

"Hey, you," Kathy yelled to Jen through the open stall door, "are you one of the hired hands?"

"Very funny," Jenny retorted, remembering the cruel comment on the first day of camp. "I didn't know you heard that."

"Ah," said Kathy, winking, "I hear everything that happens at my barn. Come on, brush that nag of yours and help me finish up. I'm *starving*."

Jenny gave Sunny a hug and then kissed her velvety nose. "Come on, sweetheart, I need to go work. You eat your lunch. I'll be back later to finish brushing you." Jenny placed a flat

feed pan in front of Sunny's nose. The horse began eating the mush mixed with corn. The girls teamed up to quickly finish the rest of the morning chores.

Jenny wolfed down lunch and returned to Sunny's stall. The mare was standing, not steadily, but she was standing. Jen stood outside the door, watching the mare pull the sweet alfalfa hay from the rack and munch. She imagined being at a big show with Sunny, winning lots of blue ribbons, trophies, and money . . .

"Jenny, hello—earth to Jenny." Kathy interrupted her lovely reverie.

"Sorry, Kathy," she replied. "I'm just thinking."

"That's all right. Hey, what is your school schedule like?"

Jenny had to stop and think for a moment. She rubbed her forehead and grimaced. School *had* seemed so far away. "Let's see, today is . . . Sunday the first of September and the first day is on Wednesday the fourth!" Jenny felt like she had been jolted back to earth. She was not ready to start school in three days, why she was just getting to know Sunny, and start a routine.

Jenny sat down on a tack trunk, suddenly depressed. She glanced at Kathy who was smiling a secret smile. "What, why are you smiling?" Jenny demanded, annoyed. "This is *not* a laughing matter," she huffed.

Kathy, still smiling, reached into her pocket to extract a very crumpled piece of paper. She handed the wad to Jenny. "Jenny Thomas, you remind me so much of myself when I was your age. I didn't really *hate* school, but I resented the time away from the horses. What you need to know is that you need to *finish* school if you ever want to do anything with horses. Showing is great, but it's expensive and you'll need to have some kind of income to finance it. Otherwise you'll wind up like me, so busy trying to make a living, that I don't have time to ride or show."

Jenny listened to Kathy, uncrumpling the paper at the same time. Her heart began racing as she read. There was a horse

show coming up Thanksgiving weekend! They had beginner classes. "Do you think I can enter this?" Jenny blurted. "Who will I ride, and what classes should I enter?"

Kathy smiled, pulling a pen from behind her ear, "Green horse/rider over fences," she said circling them in the flyer. "I think Magnum will be ready for his first show and so will you."

Suddenly school didn't seem so terrible. Kathy laughed with delight at Jenny's excitement. Jenny's whole attitude about school changed in that moment. She was actually looking forward to it starting so they could get on with the horse show. *Wait 'til my folks hear about this*, she thought.

They jogged down to the jumper barn to see Magnum. He was in the little paddock near the barn, almost as though he was waiting for them to arrive. Kathy chuckled when she saw him. "Yup, he's ready." Jenny put the leather halter on his head and led him inside. "Dr. Davis will be here any minute," said Kathy glancing at her watch. "Let's ask him to look at Sunny too."

"Great," Jen agreed. "I think I hear his truck pulling up now." The two girls began brushing Magnum together. The gelding stood patiently as the girls finished quickly.

"Howdy, ladies," greeted the vet cheerfully, tipping his cowboy hat. "How's Magnum today?" The wiry man pulled out his stethoscope and listened to Magnum's heart. Then he moved it down to listen for those important gut sounds.

"He's got good sounds in all four quadrants," Dr. Davis announced. "His eyes are bright and . . . *hey, cut that out* . . . that's *my* hat." the short man reached to remove his precious hat from Magnum's teeth, but the big animal cranked his neck all the way up near the ceiling of the barn.

"He's fine, and obviously feeling frisky," Dr. Davis continued, with a chuckle, running his fingers through his thinning white hair. "Kathy, have you got something to feed him so I can get my hat back?" he inquired.

Kathy bribed Magnum with his lunchtime grain. She poured his ration into his feed tub. He dropped the vet's hat and began eating. The vet followed Jenny toward Sunny's stall. He hadn't seen her since her bath and he kept walking after Jen stopped. He went clear to the end of the aisle before turning. "Hey, where'd she go?" he hollered to Jen.

"She's right in here," Jenny answered with a laugh.

The vet stopped outside and did a triple take. "No, that's not the same horse," he insisted.

"Yes it is," Jen said positively. "Her name is Endless Sonrise and she is a miracle horse."

"I won't argue with that," Dr. Davis agreed. "She looks great. Only time will tell if she has had permanent damage, but she looks like a different animal. Keep it up.

"Now that it looks like she'll be around for a while, let's take care of her feet. She has a condition called thrush. It's the reason her feet are so sore."

He handed Jenny a small bottle of medication for Sunny's hooves. "Apply this once a day for as long as the frog is black. Then go to every other day. Call me if you need anything else." He walked to his truck shaking his head, talking to himself.

On Monday morning, Kathy eased the saddle on Magnum's back and watched for any signs of tenderness. The big horse didn't flinch, so she went on to tighten the girth. Jen slipped the bridle over his head. She fastened all the straps and keepers and he was ready. Kathy insisted that they lunge him for a few minutes before riding. Jenny was thankful that Kathy insisted, because the quiet, sweet horse she had known was transformed into a maniac.

She watched, shocked, as he swished his long, black tail, letting out a series of bucks that would have made a bronco proud. After the bucks, he bolted to the left. Fortunately, Kathy was the one holding the long lunge line, and she didn't give an inch. After several minutes of craziness, Magnum began trot-

ting sedately. Kathy asked him to halt, then changed his direction. Magnum gave a few half-hearted bucks, but was obviously running out of steam.

"Boy, that was a show," exclaimed Jenny as she walked into the ring. "I'm really glad that you insisted on lunging. Otherwise I'd probably be picking dirt out of my teeth as we speak!"

"Actually," said Kathy, "I'm pretty sure he would *not* have done that with you on him. He just would have shied and spooked at every little thing. This way he should be relaxed and ready to go . . . slow."

Jenny put her left foot in the stirrup and swung lightly into the saddle. The horse stood like a rock. She grinned at Kathy and said, "Well, he remembered *that* lesson from before!" Magnum waited obediently for the cue from Jenny before he walked on. They walked around the ring several times in each direction. Jenny squeezed lightly and he went into his floating trot. Jenny allowed him to trot once around in each direction then brought him back to a walk.

The total workout lasted about twenty minutes. Magnum didn't even break a sweat. Jenny slid off and brought the reins over his head. Kathy nodded her approval and the threesome walked back to the barn.

The remaining two days of freedom were sweet but fleeting. Whenever Jenny found herself feeling blue about school, she reminded herself about the upcoming show.

She concentrated her efforts on training Magnum and caring for Sunny. Both horses responded, by flourishing under her gentle hand. She watched Sunny's condition improve. The mare walked normally, and her hooves no longer smelled.

It was a wondrous thing, to bring an animal back from the brink of death. Sunny was a daily reminder, to everyone at Sonrise Farm, of the incredible goodness of God.

School did start, allowing Jenny to catch up with Tessa again. Poor Tessa—she had spent her summer in Spain, which didn't sound bad, until she described it. She had been dropped off at her cousin's villa while her parents took their "separate" vacations. She had picked up some kind of intestinal bug and was sick all summer. She still looked kind of pale and skinny.

"I don't wanna hear *anything* about your summer, Jen. It'll make mine sound even crummier than it was—if that's possible," Tessa muttered at lunch.

Jenny fished her precious Sunny photos out of her backpack. They were tucked in an envelope with hearts drawn all over it. She wordlessly handed the first photo to Tessa.

"What's this?" asked Tessa, rolling her eyes at the artwork on the envelope.

"It's a picture of my horse the week we bought her," explained Jenny, whipping out a photo of Sunny.

"And who's this?" asked Tessa, eyeing the second picture, confused.

"That's the same horse last week. Her name is Endless Sonrise," said Jenny proudly.

"This isn't the same horse," Tessa declared, holding the two pictures side by side. The first photo showed a filthy horse,

on the brink of death. The other showed a thin but beautiful Palomino. It was difficult to believe, even for Jenny.

"OK, I take it back. Tell me all about your summer. I wanna hear everything," Tessa insisted.

Jenny happily obliged.

"Hey, Tess, why don't you get off the bus with me and we'll go to the barn from my house?" Jenny suggested on the way to Social Studies class.

"OK!" Tessa agreed, flashing a bright smile.

"Meetcha' on the bus," Jen shouted, ducking into her classroom.

The last class of the day was endless. *This is like torture!* Jen decided. *Will it ever end?* She couldn't wait to see Sunny again, and to show her off to Tessa.

"Here's my stop," Jenny announced later as the bus ground to a dusty stop. "Last one to the door is a rotten egg." The girls giggled in the kitchen, while Tessa dialed her mother's work number. Jenny went to her room and pulled out two pairs of sweat pants and a couple of big shirts.

"That was quick," she said when Tessa reappeared.

"Yeah," replied Tessa, "I knew she wouldn't be at her desk. I left a message on the voice mail. She probably won't hear it until after I get home anyway."

Jenny glanced at her friend and saw a flicker of pain in Tessa's eyes. Tessa smiled a wry smile, then began picking up the sweats, trying to decide which ones accented her hair.

Mrs. Thomas pulled up at Sonrise Farm and the girls bounced out of the car like a red-and-black tumbleweed. They grinned and waved as they ran up to the barn. Mrs. Thomas poked her head out of the car window and called, "I'll pick you up in two hours!" She smiled as Jenny glanced at her watch and waved an affirmative.

"I can't wait for you to see Sunny and Magnum and the other horses that I've been riding all summer," Jenny said excitedly. They walked past the empty stalls and as Jenny approached Sunny's stall, she saw that it, too, was empty. "Now that's strange," she thought aloud.

They went around the barn to the first paddock, and there was Sunny. That could only mean that Kathy thought Sunny was strong enough to handle being outside all day! It was a huge milestone in Sunny's recovery.

Sunny stood dozing, in the September sunshine. Her head popped up when the gate rattled. She pricked her ears and nickered loudly as she walked toward the girls.

"Oh Jenny, she is beautiful!" exclaimed Tessa. "She's still skinny, but her face is gorgeous, and . . . how tall *is* she?"

"She is 17 hands," Jenny said, proudly.

"Wow." Tessa stopped talking to Jenny and stood rubbing Sunny's neck. Tessa seemed lost in thought as she murmured softly to the mare. Jenny walked around the corner to the tack room and pulled out a box of brushes. Sunny stood quietly as the girls brushed and curried her from head to toe.

Kathy came "Yoo hooing" out of the house. Jenny introduced Kathy and Tessa again, though they remembered each other from summer camp. It just seemed like so much had happened since then.

Jenny left Tessa with Sunny and went to work on Magnum. Kathy retrieved the bay gelding from the field while Jenny laid the necessary tack out in the aisle. By the time Tessa finished grooming Sunny, Jenny was walking Magnum around the ring for the third time.

Tessa ambled toward the ring and sat on the hard, green, wooden bleacher next to Kathy. The girls watched Jenny as she worked the leggy bay. Magnum and Jenny were lovely to see. Jenny sat relaxed but straight, her head up, but not stiff.

Her hands were light, yet firm. She sat about as perfectly as someone could.

Magnum responded by walking briskly and powerfully with his back round and relaxed. His sensitive ears flicked back and forth as he listened for the voice of his rider. Jenny gave Magnum a gentle squeeze, and he broke into his elegant trot. They floated around the ring once and then again. Jenny pulled lightly on the inside rein guiding the horse in a large circle until they had changed directions. They walked on a long rein for a few moments, then began trotting again.

Jenny squeezed with her outside leg, and Magnum popped into a choppy canter. It was a bumpy ride, but Jenny stayed relaxed until the big gelding was able to smooth himself out. As soon as Magnum had given her a couple of nice canter strides, Jenny pulled him up and patted him profusely. He seemed pleased with himself and began dancing a sideways jig. Magnum grabbed the bit, pulling excitedly on the reins. He shook his head and gave a tiny rear. He felt good and wanted to keep going!

"No you don't, silly boy," Jenny crooned, sitting quietly on his quivering back. She was not frightened. These were all good signs that he had fully recovered. Magnum settled under her quiet hands and walked peacefully around the ring to the gate. Jenny swung her lithe body out of the saddle, landing lightly on her feet. The horse pushed her playfully with his big head as she walked through the gate in front of him.

"Hey, stop that you big galoot," she laughed. It was a cute trick, but not one that she wanted him to continue. They walked to the bleachers where Kathy and Tessa sat. Jenny was surprised to see Tessa looking at her with awe. "What? What's the deal? Why are you guys staring at me?"

Tessa said nothing, and Kathy just smiled. Jenny huffed her disapproval and started back to the barn, leading Magnum. Tessa chased her down and began relating what Kathy had told her during Jenny's ride. "Jenny . . . I swear, Kathy told me that you had more talent than anyone she has ever seen, and that you are going to be a world class rider some day."

"No way, Tessa. There is no way she said that," Jenny snorted.

"Well," replied Tessa quietly. "We'll just have to wait and see, won't we?"

The rest of September and the month of October were almost too good to be true. Jenny established a routine at home and school that allowed her to spend her precious afternoons at the barn. She was amazed at how much homework she could finish before she left school, and anything she didn't accomplish there she finished right off the bus.

Rumors began to spread at school about Jenny's horse and how she was becoming a "brain." The funny thing was that now some of the popular girls wanted to spend time with Jenny. She was apologetic but firm. She had to finish her homework!

Sunny's condition continued to improve and by the end of October no one would have believed she was the same animal from the auction. Even Dr. Davis was amazed.

He stopped by one late October afternoon to vaccinate some of the weanlings. When he ran into Jen at the school barn, he watched Jenny brush Sunny for a few moments. "Hey, Miss Jenny," he called, "how's that mare you bought?"

"You're looking at her," replied Jenny, watching him closely again. Jenny was not disappointed. The veterinarian was astonished. He insisted upon a complete exam, at no charge, and proclaimed Sunny healthy and sound.

"I would get another 100 pounds on her before winter," he said, smiling to a thrilled Jenny. "I would start working her next month. But take it slow and easy."

"We will," Jenny promised.

Thanksgiving held an entirely new meaning for Jenny. The Thomas family and several other families from church met at the pastor's house. Everybody brought something for the table. It was a boisterous, joyful time of fellowship. There were usually at least ten small noisy children running underfoot. After the gigantic meal, all the family members lounged around the crackling fireplace to share what they were thankful for.

Tessa came with Jenny because her mother was out-of-town again, and Mr. Shields, not feeling particularly thankful, had gone golfing. Tessa phoned Jen, mostly to complain, and got invited to the gathering. She looked a little uncomfortable at first, but the warmth of the group was contagious. Before long, she, too, shared something she felt thankful for.

Jenny usually felt awkward when speaking to a group. Well, this year she could not wait to talk about what God was doing in her life. She shared her testimony, and a short version of the Magnum crisis. Sunny's story brought the whole room to tears. Jenny caught Tessa's eye and was surprised to see tears shining there.

The day ended reluctantly as families tore themselves away.

Jenny gave a general invitation to the show, and two of the families promised to attend.

Am I ready? she wondered. *Is Magnum?*

Show day began with a crash. Jenny woke to thunder and pouring rain. She sat up, thinking about how hard she had worked. She headed for the kitchen. Her folks were sitting together, having their Bible study. Jenny lingered in the hallway just outside the door of the kitchen feeling like an intruder on a private moment. "Come on in Jenny," her dad called. "Join us."

Mom brought Jenny a plate and some utensils. "Would you like some cocoa, Jen?"

"Sure, that would be great."

As Mom made cocoa, Dad asked the dreaded question. "So, are we going to the show today?"

"I don't know," Jenny replied bleakly. "I'll have to call Kathy and ask her. I'll do it a little later, when I am sure she is awake." They sat in silence sipping their drinks.

The phone jangled once and Jenny choked on her drink. She exploded from the table, spilling cocoa onto the linoleum.

"Hello. Thomas residence, Jenny speaking," she announced, crossing her fingers. "Hi," answered a deep, masculine voice. "This is John Jamison, is Mike Thomas there, please?"

"Sure," Jenny replied, trying not to sound disappointed. "Dad, it's for you."

"Don't look so glum," Dad said as he gently patted her cheek. "This may be a job for me, which means food for you."

Jenny heard her father talking and could tell by his voice that it was indeed a job. He strode into the kitchen positively glowing. "Well, it's happening, we have just been offered our first big contract. We'll be working on a new library in town."

"Mike, that is wonderful," Mom said, almost as happy as he was.

Jenny squeezed her dad, really hard, around the middle. "That's great Dad," she said proudly. "You deserve it."

The phone rang again. Dad answered. "Jen, it's for you. It's Kathy."

"Hey, Kathy, what do you think?" Jenny asked anxiously. Her mouth went dry as Kathy hesitated.

"Jenny, the show is indoors, but we have to park and unload outside. If it stays like this, it's probably not a good idea. If it stops thundering and lightning, we'll go. We have a couple of hours, so let's just relax and see what happens. I'll call you at nine o'clock and let you know what I think. In the meantime, eat some breakfast and take it easy. I'll talk to you soon."

Jenny hung up muttering. *Eat and relax. Yeah right,* she thought. She decided to make a list of what she would need to do before the show—if they went. Her hands trembled and she felt shaky. She almost wished it would start pouring again. At least then, she would *know* what was happening. Her folks waited in the kitchen. They held hands as Dad said grace.

"Heavenly Father, we thank You for Your grace and mercy. We thank You for providing this food. Thank You for this family and Your provision for all our needs. Please keep us safe as we go about our business today. Make our lives be a witness to Your goodness. Amen."

"Amen," echoed Jenny and Mom in harmony.

By nine o'clock it had stopped raining, though it was still gray outside. Kathy called as promised, and they decided to give it a try. Jenny snatched the pack containing her sweats and boots and climbed into the station wagon. They arrived at Sonrise Farm and walked up the little rise toward the jumper barn.

They could see Kathy standing in the doorway of the yellow house. Mom gave Jenny a quick hug. "Your dad and I will see you in a couple of hours at the show," she said, starting back to the car. Jenny nodded, waving goodbye.

Gazing out at the expanse of pasture reminded Jenny of the glorious dream she used to have. The grass was shiny wet, and steam rose from the ground. It looked almost magical. The dream fields she and the Palomino stallion had galloped across had looked very much like these. She realized that she hadn't thought about the stallion in a long time, and had not missed him. *Perhaps I am living my dreams,* she mused.

Then she returned to reality with a start. *The show! I need to get Magnum ready!* Jenny rushed into the jumper barn. Magnum waited patiently in his stall, perfectly groomed, by whom? Someone had even braided his mane! He looked gorgeous. Jenny heard a noise and spun around to see the O'Rileys smiling at her from the doorway.

"He looks fabulous," whispered Jenny gratefully. "Thank you for braiding him."

"Thank my dad," returned Kathy. "He got up extra early to do it."

"Thank you, Mr. O'Riley," Jenny said shyly. "He looks beautiful."

"You are welcome, Jennifer," he boomed in his deep Irish brogue. "Here, we would like you to have this also."

He gently handed Jenny a long, deep box wrapped in red paper. She gave a little gasp, then crouched on the stoop of the tack room to open it. She gazed up into their smiling faces. "What's this for?" she asked, trembling.

"Just open it, you goose," Kathy laughed.

Jenny tore into the paper, and with quaking fingers managed to open the top. Inside lay a pair of tan britches, a ratcatcher, and two tall, black, shiny leather boots.

Jen's eyes welled up with tears, and she felt like she was going to weep. Kathy plopped down next to her, placing a warm arm around her back. "You didn't think I was going to let you show our most promising horse in sweats and work boots, did you? You are representing Sonrise Farm and you have to look the part. Consider these your show uniform. They come with the job."

Mrs. O'Riley bustled over and gave Jenny a warm hug. Jenny could smell rosewater and woodstove smoke in her hair. "Good luck today, Little Jenny," she murmured. Wiping one pink cheek on the corner of her apron, Mrs. O'Riley headed back to the house. Mr. O'Riley gave Magnum a final pat on the neck, then wished Jenny God speed.

Jenny thanked him again and set about getting the big horse ready to go. "That's what I like about you, Jenny," Kathy chuckled. "You're all business when it comes to the horses." Jenny shrugged and continued her work, but inside she was glowing.

The girls loaded Magnum onto the trailer. He walked on like an old campaigner. Kathy brought the saddle; Jenny grabbed the bridle and the box with her new clothes. They jumped into the truck and were off!

* * *

At Hunter's Ridge, Kathy checked the hay net in the trailer to make sure the gelding had plenty to munch, then they marched to the office to register. Jenny scanned the parking lot, amazed by the number of trailers. There had to be a hundred of them, some from as far away as North Carolina. She glanced at Kathy who hummed a little tune, unfazed by the situation. Jenny shrugged her shoulders and tried to ignore it also.

The line for registration seemed endless, and by the time they arrived at the table, Jenny had a throbbing headache. She entered in the novice jumping class. If everything went according to schedule, they'd be finished by one o'clock.

Kathy peeked into the registration envelope and pulled out Jenny's number. She held it up in front of her as though it were a newspaper, and announced, "And the winner is . . . number 75, Jenny Thomas, riding the elegant Magnum Force."

Jenny giggled, delighted and embarrassed. With about forty minutes to go, she snatched her clothes and headed for the ladies room to change. The britches were perfect, the boots a little big. Jenny jogged back to the trailer to help put the finishing touches on Magnum.

"Let me see," fussed Kathy, adjusting Jenny's ratcatcher. "How does everything feel? Are you comfortable? Pretend you're sitting on a horse. How are the britches?"

"Everything is great Kathy, except the boots are a little big."

"Take them off and put on these woolly socks. They will take up the extra room . . . hopefully. Those were my boots, from my first days of showing," Kathy said wistfully, as she helped Jenny pull the boots off. The socks worked, the boots fit just fine. Kathy pinned Jenny's number on her jacket and helped her put it on. "Well, Jenny," declared Kathy. "You look like a picture—in fact, say cheese." Kathy pulled a camera out of her pocket and snapped a photo.

Jenny placed her foot in the stirrup, gave one hop and swung gracefully onto Magnum's back. He gave a tiny sidestep, then walked with quick, choppy strides toward the warm-up ring.

Unfortunately, the warm-up area was chaos. Horses and riders galloped madly around. In the center of the tiny ring was a three-foot crossrail, which horses were popping over. Jenny witnessed three near collisions and decided to avoid the area. Magnum was alert and as stiff as a plank. His head was up, ears pricked, intelligent eyes taking in the whole scene.

He shied suddenly at a yapping dog, but quickly corrected. He shook his head almost as if to chastise himself for being so silly.

Jenny patted him on the neck, murmuring soothing words. They made it to the lower ring without any other breaches of etiquette. Jenny tried to calm the butterflies in her stomach. She did not want to transmit *her* anxiety to the already nervous horse. She recalled Kathy's words about relaxing: "Remember Jenny, horses can't actually smell fear. What they react to is the stiffness in your hands and back. Breathe . . . relax, and you will both feel better."

Jenny took a deep breath, then scrunched her shoulders up to her ears. *Yeah, I'm stiff too.* She felt a sudden impulse to whisper a prayer. "Father, thank You for getting us this far. Please keep us safe and relaxed. Amen."

Jenny felt relaxed and ready. Her mount responded just as Kathy had said he would. Magnum relaxed his back, lowered his head and sighed. He became round and responsive in her hands. Jenny quickly found herself thinking only of riding Magnum as they found their natural balance and harmony. She barely noticed her parents standing with Kathy at the fence.

A crackly whine penetrated Jenny's concentration. Her head snapped up, listening intently as her class was called. She patted Magnum's glossy muscled neck with her gloved hand, "Here we go, boy." The bay's black-tipped ears flicked back at the sound of her voice. He surged forward eagerly, and they trotted toward the huge indoor arena. Jenny's class was packed with riders, so she and Magnum waited outside the massive sliding doors. Jenny felt herself getting apprehensive again and she tried to relax. Magnum stood quietly, chewing the fat snaffle bit, watching the other horses.

"Number 75, Jennifer Thomas on Magnum Force," yelped the loudspeaker.

Jenny took a deep breath and squeezed her leg. She stroked Magnum softly as they approached the formidable gates. Magnum hesitated before entering the dark building, but Jenny closed her leg and he went forward obediently.

They passed the exiting horse walking through the red metal gate. It clanged loudly behind them, causing Magnum to tuck his tail and rush forward. Jenny sat deep and collected him.

Jen saluted the judge and the bell tinkled. *Relax,* she said to herself. Magnum took a few quick steps, then settled into a working trot. Jenny posted while scanning the nine jumps in the ring.

Each jump was two-foot-three. There were four red and white oxers, two walls, and three brush jumps. Magnum and Jenny had practiced on jumps up to two-foot-nine, but only on the plain schooling standards at Sonrise Farm. These jumps *looked* bigger, brighter, and scarier.

Magnum pricked his ears as he trotted easily over the first oxer. The wall caused him to hesitate, but Jenny nudged him and he popped it. Jenny lurched forward onto his neck but regained her balance quickly. They trotted on to the first brush jump. Jenny could feel Magnum's apprehension as they approached. *Leg. Leg. Leg,* she thought. His stride smoothed, and they sailed over. The second oxer felt like an old friend, and the rest of the round was clean.

They cantered to the finish line, then walked out. Jenny could hear nothing except the roaring blood in her ears as her heart pounded wildly. She slapped Magnum's sweaty neck enthusiastically realizing what they had done. A clean round, in an indoor arena, over jumps he had never seen before. Incredible!

Back at the trailer, Jenny threw Magnum's show sheet over his back, saddle and all. She felt more nervous now than she had before they went in. *Take a deep breath,* she said to her-

self. "Magnum, you were awesome," she said, congratulating the young gelding.

Kathy and her parents converged on them, patting Jenny and Magnum vigorously. "You looked great," Kathy crowed. "Get back on, the jump off will be in about ten minutes."

"Jump off? What jump off? What are you talking about?" Jenny asked, her voice quavering.

"Uh oh . . . Didn't I explain the jump-off part? Sorry. Well, all the riders who had a clean round come back and jump a timed course. The fastest clean round wins. The jumps will be higher, but there will be fewer. It's all right," Kathy assured her. "The class is huge so you have a few minutes. The important thing is to keep Magnum moving so he doesn't get stiff. Use your judgment, and remember, this is just a schooling show. Its purpose is to prepare you both for real shows."

"If it's *just* a schooling show, why am I so nervous?" Jenny complained.

"Because you are a natural competitor," Kathy laughed. "Do your best, and put the rest in God's hands. We'll meet you back here when you finish."

Jenny found a relatively quiet place to walk and trot. Entering the warm-up ring was still a risky venture. Jenny's butterflies began to reappear as she waited for the announcement of the jump-off.

There it was. "Number 87, Lisa Johnson, riding Rainbow's End. Number 75, Jenny Thomas, on deck." Jenny guided Magnum to the tiny wait area known as "the deck."

"Breathe . . . breathe," mouthed Kathy from the sidelines.

Jenny sucked in a deep breath. It felt tight and unnatural.

Lisa and the gray pony crashed into the first brush jump and were out of contention. Jenny watched, horrified, as Lisa savagely struck her pony with her crop. She yanked on the gray's mouth and departed the arena in tears.

"Number 75. Jenny Thomas on Magnum Force," whined

the loudspeaker in Jenny's ear. They stepped through the metal gate, trotted to the judge's stand, stopped and saluted. The bell tinkled and the clock started.

Jenny turned Magnum around, scanning the course. The jumps had been raised to two-foot-six, but there were only five of them. She urged Magnum into a rolling canter and they flew over the first oxer. He pricked his ears but did not hesitate as he cleared the brush jump. A tight turn, a wall, one more oxer, then an outrageously decorated brush jump. They galloped to the finish line and out the gate. *That was great,* thought Jenny, *fast and fun.*

"That was great," echoed Kathy. "I am proud of both of you. Now we just have to wait and see if anyone beats your time in the jump-off. I'll tell you a secret. I used to do these jumper shows on Poppet. We usually won. You guys beat my best time by two seconds."

Stunned, Jenny turned and stared at Kathy. "Wha . . . what? How is that possible?" she stammered.

"Easy, you guided Magnum around the course in the most efficient way. You did not take one extra step. You kept a consistent speed and you had no refusals. Believe it or not Jenny, you are the most talented rider I have ever seen. Your instincts are incredible. Magnum is the best we have bred at Sonrise Farm, and together you are great."

Jenny stood processing this shocking information when her folks rushed up. Jenny was just about to tell them what Kathy had told her when Dad engulfed her in a gigantic hug. "You beat the next best rider by three seconds Jenny!" he crowed releasing her. "You won the jump-off!"

Jenny felt so dizzy she had to lean against Magnum for support. He turned his big face toward her, nuzzling her pocket for a treat. She fished one out and handed it to him, then glanced at her mom. "Good job, Jenny," exclaimed Mom. "We are so proud of you."

"Thanks, Mom, Dad, and Kathy. I couldn't have done it without you. And you, Magnum." She patted him heartily on his muscled neck. Sweat had dried, leaving crusty lines in his hair. Jenny used her fingers to loosen the salt and brush away the residue. She gazed at Magnum's gentle face. He was beginning to doze, his big brown eyes closing slowly. "Well, at least someone is calm about all of this," she giggled.

Kathy gave her a leg up and Jenny rode back to collect her blue ribbon. It was amazing. She knew in her head that she had won—her dad had told her so. It was her pounding heart that was not convinced.

She sat in the saddle, coiling one tiny lock around her finger. The rest of her hair was safe, piled in her helmet. She heard the announcer. "Third place goes to . . . Jennifer Rhoads, riding Desert Summer." Jenny heard the name and started forward before realizing it was a different Jennifer. She stopped and looked around self-consciously.

"Second place goes to . . . Patricia Keener, riding Merlin's Magic." Patricia obviously had a large fan club with her and they burst into a frenzy of clapping and cheering. Merlin's Magic did not appreciate the outburst and reared. Patricia kicked him, forcing him to walk on, and managed to collect her red ribbon without coming off.

"And the winner of the novice class in the first division is Jennifer Thomas . . . riding Magnum Force." Everyone in the arena applauded wildly. Magnum jigged sideways nervously as the echo bounced from wall to wall.

Jenny gazed around at the people in the bleachers. Everyone was standing and clapping vigorously. *What on earth?* she thought.

"Ms. Thomas and Magnum Force went around this course faster than any other novice horse and rider in the history of this series," crackled the loudspeaker. "I expect we will be see-

ing more of these two in the future. Congratulations, Ms. Thomas and Sonrise Farm."

Jenny squeezed Magnum forward as the judge walked toward her with the blue ribbon. He stared into Jenny's eyes with a piercing gaze. It felt as though he could look right through her thoughts. He glanced down as he placed the ribbon into Magnum's bridle. Reaching up to Jenny, he stuck out his hand to shake, grinning at her. "It is my *extreme* pleasure to present you with this gift certificate from Rider's Saddlery and to say, well done. I *do* expect to see you both in the winner's circle again . . . soon."

Jenny guided Magnum out of the ring in a daze. She glanced at the gift certificate. It was in the amount of $100. *Wow, what am I going to buy with 100 dollars?* she mused. She knew . . . a bridle for Sunny. *She'll be rideable soon and we are going to need a bridle.* "Thank You, Lord," she whispered.

Back at the barn, Jenny finished her chores quickly, then went to visit Sunny. The mare walked over, gently nuzzling Jenny's pockets. Jenny gazed at Sunny's lovely face, then slipped Sunny's halter on and tied her to the fence. Jenny fetched her brushes and began grooming Sunny's now shiny coat.

Jenny had a hard time feeling the mare's ribs as she brushed. She curried the horse from head to toe, then stood back to admire her work. In three months Sunny had returned to a normal looking . . . no . . . a drop-dead gorgeous horse.

Kathy leaned over the fence to watch. "Hey, Jen," she called. "Let's tack up that nag of yours and see what she can do."

Jenny's head popped up, and she stared at Kathy in disbelief. Her paralysis was momentary. She bolted to the tack room and grabbed a saddle and bridle. Her fingers felt thick and heavy. She did not think she would ever finish. Sunny stood patiently allowing Jenny to tighten the girth. Finally, she was done.

Kathy picked up the lunge line and whip as they headed for the ring. Once in the ring, Kathy took over as Jenny stood near the rail of the fence. Kathy gave Sunny about two feet of slack in the lunge line and carefully placed the long whip right behind the mare's flaxen tail.

Sunny snorted and took a couple of hopping steps, then realized she was not being hit with the whip. Her strides became long and loose. She was elegant to watch. What a difference from the summer! Kathy asked her to walk for ten minutes and then clucked her tongue and said, "Trot."

Sunny continued walking, though it was faster. Kathy tried again. "TUR-OT, come on Sunny, give us a trot." The mare did not respond.

Jenny walked to Sunny's head. When Kathy gave the command to trot, Jenny trotted around the ring, leading the mare. After three times of practicing the transition, Sunny obeyed on her own. Jenny released the bridle and stood back to watch. She did it! *What a smart girl,* thought Jenny. Kathy put the lunge line on Sunny's right side and repeated the exercise. This time when Kathy said, "tur-ot," the mare picked up the trot immediately.

Kathy worked Sunny for a total of twenty minutes. She mostly walked and received praise for being so clever. They headed back to the barn as the sun was beginning to go down. It had been a long and exhilarating day for everyone.

Kathy fed the hungry horses while Jenny filled water buckets and threw hay into the racks. When they finished, Kathy leaned back against the barn, chewing a piece of hay thoughtfully, "Jenny, before either of us gets on Sunny, I would like to have a friend of my father's ride her . . . just in case. We don't need to be getting bucked off and hurt. This guy is a professional trainer. He would probably do it for free if I have my dad ask him. What do you think of that idea?"

Jenny fought to hide her dismay. She had envisioned being the first one to ride Sunny, though she had to admit, the idea of being bucked off wasn't fun.

"OK," she agreed reluctantly, "But I want to be here when he rides."

"Of course," Kathy agreed. "I wouldn't do that to you. I'll ask my dad tonight."

Kathy and Jenny walked into the farmhouse together. Kathy found her father and asked him to call Bill Bowman. Mr. O'Riley agreed that this was the safest route, since nobody really knew Sunny. He looked through his Rolodex and found the number. The girls sat at the table, watching intently.

"Hello, Bill?" he said after a moment. "How are you? Haven't seen much of you lately. Listen . . . I have a favor to ask. One of Kathy's students bought a horse at the bloodstock auction, you know, the one in August. Anyway, she bought a Thoroughbred mare in pretty bad shape. We've been fattening her up and rehabilitating her. She is now ready for some work, but I don't want these girls getting hurt. Would you ride her for us, just once, to see what she is like? I would really appreciate it . . . Thanks, I owe you one."

The girls cheered and gave each other a high five. "He'll be out tomorrow," said Mr. O'Riley. "He said to expect him around 2:30."

"Perfect," crowed Jenny. "I'll come over right after lunch."

🐎 🐎 🐎

The air at the barn was filled with expectation as Jenny placed the saddle on Sunny. She tightened the girth, then threw her arms around Sunny's neck. The mare nuzzled her gently as Jenny stroked the golden face.

A four-wheel drive truck rumbled slowly up the driveway. Everyone turned to see who it was. It was Bill Bowman. He climbed out of the truck and ambled to the barn area. Bill was a tall, lean man, with wiry legs. He had lots of blond hair under a worn 10-gallon hat, and his face was adorned with a big handlebar mustache. He looked like a caricature of a cowboy. He even wore faded blue jeans and cowboy boots. Why ... he actually was a cowboy.

Mr. O'Riley strode over and the two men shook hands warmly. "Here she is," he boomed, introducing Sunny. "Her name is Sunny and she has been nothing but good since she came here. This is Jenny Thomas the owner, and these good people are Jenny's parents, Mike and Judy Thomas."

"Howdy, folks," said Bill, the cowboy, tipping his hat. "Well," he went on in a slow drawl, "Tell me what else you do know about this mare before I get on her." He walked slowly around Sunny, looking her up and down, nodding approvingly.

"Jenny bought her at the bloodstock auction this summer," explained Kathy. "We have been feeding her and taking care of her feet for over three months. Jenny and I tried lunging her yesterday, but she didn't really know what we were up to."

"She is really smart though," Jenny blurted. "She did better after we showed her what to do."

Everyone stared at Jenny. She felt the danger signs mounting. Hot face, tingly eyes, dry swollen throat. She was going to lose it. Maybe she should let Kathy and Mr. O'Riley take care of this.

"I was at the bloodstock auction," Bill said slowly, "and I didn't see this horse."

"Well, she didn't look like this when we bought her," Jenny spouted. "She was starved and really dirty and . . . and . . ." *Why am I getting so upset?* she wondered.

Kathy explained the condition Sunny had been in when Jenny bought her, and what they had done to rehabilitate her.

"Ahh," said Bill quietly, "I guess I *did* see this horse. Well, you young ladies have certainly done a beautiful job with her. I would never have guessed this was the same mare, never in a million years." He turned and winked kindly at Jenny. "Now, let's get the show on the road." He unclipped Sunny's halter and she followed him like a lamb. The group marched down to the ring, a nervous Jenny in tow. Bill led

Sunny into the ring, and Jenny sprinted to close the gate behind them.

The cowboy patted Sunny's sleek neck, shaking his head in disbelief. Jenny perched on the top rail of the fence, watching Bill like a hawk. "Please, God, let Sunny be OK," she whispered over and over. Her concern now was for the safety of her horse . . . well . . . and Bill, sort of.

Bill pulled the stirrups down, checking the length. They needed to be longer so he pulled the top part of the leather until the buckle showed. He made the leathers about four holes longer and did the same on the opposite side. Then he patted Sunny's neck again and gracefully swung himself up onto her back. He did it so quickly that everyone was surprised, including Sunny. She sidestepped a little, snorting and blowing. Bill gathered the reins as they started around the ring.

Jenny watched as Sunny began walking faster and faster. Gone were the loose, relaxed strides from the day before. The mare's neck was stiff, her back hollow. Bill responded by taking a tighter hold on the reins. Sunny reacted by breaking into a canter.

Moments later Sunny was thundering wildly around the ring with Bill standing in the stirrups, see-sawing the bit through Sunny's mouth.

Stop pulling on her! Stop it, Jenny's pounding heart screamed.

Without thinking, Jenny jumped off the fence into Sunny's path. She knew that if she could just touch the mare, Sunny would stop. Kathy and Mom gasped simultaneously, racing to grab her. It was too late. Sunny lurched to a halt at Jen's side. The mare stood, drenched and trembling for a moment, then placed her quivering nose under Jenny's arm.

Bill leaped off and handed the reins to Jenny. He was clearly embarrassed, but managed to stay calm. "This mare has been

horribly abused by someone," Bill exclaimed. "She is not misbehaving; she is truly terrified. I recommend selling her to someone who can really work with her, like a professional trainer. She is one of the strongest horses I have ever ridden. She could out muscle any rider on the planet. She is really not a suitable mount for a young lady."

Jenny listened carefully, nodding occasionally. "Thank you very much, Mr. Bowman," she whispered, her heart sinking. Jenny turned and led Sunny toward the gate. Her shoulders felt unbearably heavy. Jenny looked up to see her mother's stricken face. Even Dad was crying. As Jenny fumbled with the gate latch, a ridiculous idea came to her. Sunny nudged her in agreement. The adults were walking, hunched and miserable, back to the barn.

"What would happen if I just sat on you, Sunny girl?" she crooned. Jenny kept talking to the mare in a quiet, singsong voice. She approached Sunny's side and placed her foot in the stirrup. Sunny turned her head to watch. Jenny gave one tiny hop and was up!

The stirrups were still adjusted for Mike Bowman's long legs, so Jenny crossed them in front of her. "We don't want these old things scaring you, do we, girl?" Jenny sang. The horse and girl walked around the ring. Jenny kept her fingers soft and pliable. When Sunny pulled at the reins, Jenny gave her slack. When Sunny became stiff, Jenny relaxed her own back and patted the mare reassuringly. It worked! Sunny sauntered around the ring like a trail horse.

Jenny's dad, halfway to the barn, turned to see where Jenny had gone and gasped. Everyone else turned and stared with open mouths at the ring.

Jenny urged Sunny into a trot. *Lovely. Floaty.* She sat deep and relaxed her back. Sunny came back to a walk. She urged her into a trot, then a canter. *Beautiful transition.*

The mare showed no sign of fear. Jenny released the reins

and stuck her arms straight out. She was flying! Tears flowed freely and were whipped away. Her heart felt like it would burst. *I will wake up any moment*. . .she thought. Then Jenny heard voices calling, screaming . . .

"Jennifer Lynn Thomas, you stop that horse . . . now!"

It took a moment for Jenny's eyes to focus. Mom stood at the gate, hands on hips. Jenny rarely heard that tone of voice from her mother and she obeyed. She relaxed her back and sat deep. Sunny slowed to a walk in just a few strides.

"Mom, Kathy, I'm sorry, I wasn't thinking . . . I knew she wouldn't be scared of me. I just *knew* I could ride her. I didn't think about how you would feel."

"Jenny, I want you to be safe. You're not even wearing a helmet! Do not EVER get on any horse again without one. Do you hear me?"

Jenny's hand flew to her head. She hadn't thought of the helmet. "I promise Mom," she agreed, sliding down Sunny's side. She hugged the mare's golden neck. "I RODE HER!" she crowed.

They headed back to the barn. Sunny placed her nose between Jenny's shoulder blades and followed her, like a foal follows its mama. Jenny felt her heart pulse with a love that bound her and the big mare together. For always.

Thank You, Father. It is more than I ever dreamed. More than I ever dreamed.

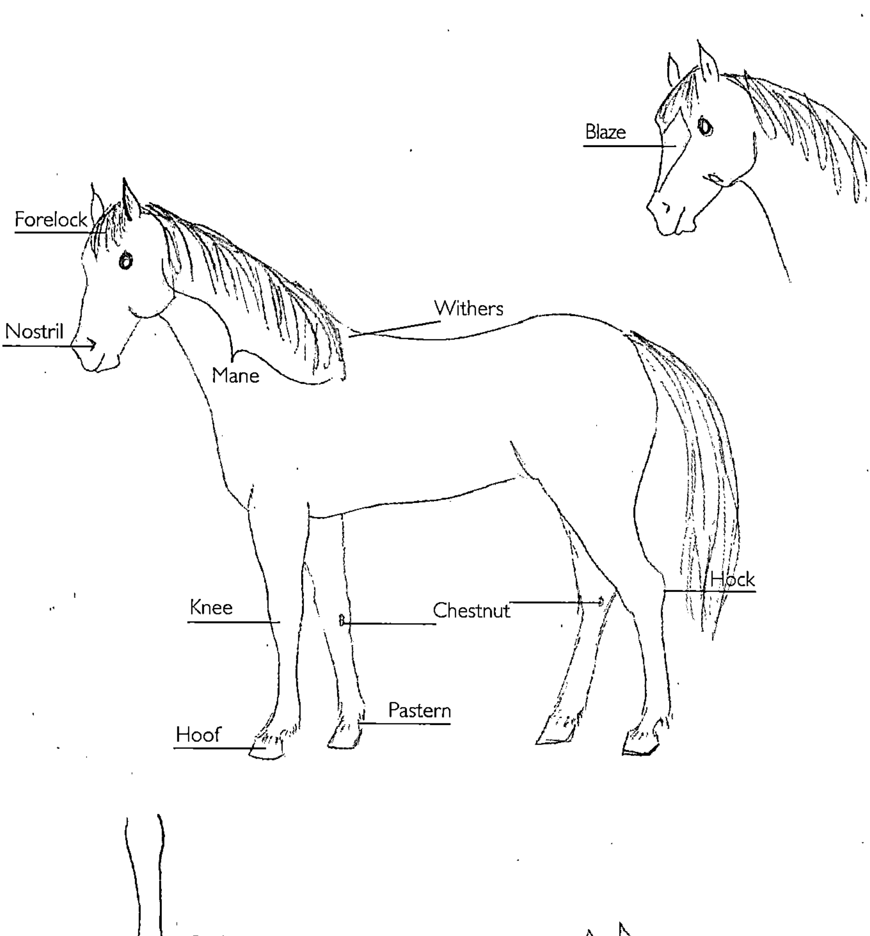
Blaze
Forelock
Nostril
Mane
Withers
Knee
Chestnut
Hock
Hoof
Pastern

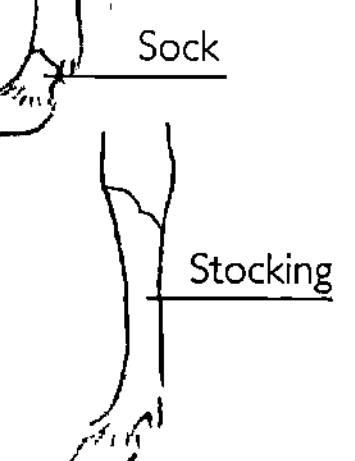
Sock
Stocking

Star
Snip

Glossary

A

Arabian—An ancient breed of horse from the deserts of Arabia. Arabians are known for their courage, stamina, and beauty.

B

Bay—A color term for a brown horse whose points (bottom part of legs, mane, and tail) are black. Bays may range from a medium brown to almost black (called a seal bay). A red horse with black points is called a blood bay.

Bridle—The leather straps that fit onto the horse's head to keep the bit in place. The bit is the metal part that goes through the horse's mouth. The reins are the connection to the rider.

Broodmare—A female horse whose job is to have foals (baby horses).

Buckskin—A color term for a light brown horse whose points are black. The color of the body may range from a deep gold to sandy. Buckskins may also have a dorsal stripe (a stripe that runs from wither to tail).

C

Canter—One of the four gaits of a horse. Walk, trot, canter, then gallop. Canter is a three-beat gait, usually smooth and easy to ride.

Chestnut—A color term for a plain red horse.

Clydesdale—One of America's most popular draft (working) horses. Clydesdales are huge, (18 hands or more) powerful work horses used for hauling heavy carts or farm machin-

ery. They are usually bay or black in color, with "feathers" (long hair) covering their hooves.

Colic—A term used to describe stomachache in horses. Colic can be deadly serious or simply a bout of gas that passes on its own.

Colt—A young male horse.

Curry comb—A hard rubber brush used to remove deep or caked-on dirt. It should be used vigorously but carefully, because it is hard. It is not used on the lower part of the legs, nor on the face. Once the dirt has been brought to the surface and loosened, it can be brushed away by the softer bristled body brush.

E

Equine—Scientific name for horses and ponies.

Euthanize—Medical term for destroying an animal. It is usually performed by injecting a deadly substance into the vein. The animal goes to sleep and never wakes. It is painless and fast.

F

Filly—A young female horse.

Foal—A baby horse of either sex.

G

Gelding—A castrated (neutered) male horse. Most male horses in the U.S. are geldings. Only horses intended for breeding are maintained as stallions.

Girth—A leather or fabric belt used to keep the saddle on the horse's back. The girth attaches to both sides of the saddle under the belly of the horse.

Grand Prix—The highest level of competitive show jumping.

Green—An untrained horse.

H

Hands—A measurement term for horses and ponies. Each hand equals four inches. The horse is measured from the ground to the withers (see parts of the horse diagram). A pony who measures ten hands would be forty inches tall at the withers.

Hoofpick—A hand-sized pick used to remove dirt from the inside of a horse's hoof.

Horse—An equine who measures at least 14'2 hands. That is: fourteen hands and two inches. An animal who measures 14'2 would be 58 inches at the withers, or 4 feet, 8 inches. At 17 hands Magnum and Sunny stand 5 foot 8 inches at the withers.

I

Impaction—A serious form of colic where something (food or foreign object) blocks the digestive tract.

Inside and Outside reins—A term used to describe the reins as the horse is moving in a circle. Imagine that you are standing in the center of a ring. There is someone riding clockwise around you. The right side of the horse and rider is visible to you. This is the "inside." The left side of the horse and rider is visible from the fence. This is the "outside." If the horse were to change directions, then the left side would be "inside."

M

Mare—An adult female horse.

Morgan—A small strong American breed of horse descended from Justin Morgan's famous little bay stallion of the late 1700s.

Mucking Out—Cleaning a stall.

N

Nicker—A low chuckling sound horses make when they see someone or something they love.

P

Paddock—A small enclosure, usually less than an acre in size.

Palomino—A color breed whose coat is the color of a newly minted gold coin. The mane and tail should be platinum.

Platinum—A precious metal that is almost white in color.

Post—The action of rising and sitting in the saddle while your mount is trotting. The reason for posting during the trot is to reduce the jarring that occurs.

R

Ratcatcher—A shirt worn when showing. It has a high collar that gathers around the neck and is secured with a pin.

Registered—Each individual breed of horse and pony has a registry, or a list of its members. The registered horses can then trace their ancestry. The Jockey Club of America also requires all racing Thoroughbreds to be tattooed on the inside of the upper lip. This stands as permanent proof of a horse's identity. Sunny, being tattooed, is a registered Thoroughbred. All Jenny needs to do to find Sunny's bloodlines is call the Jockey Club and tell them the number on Sunny's lip. They will be able to look up Sunny's bloodlines.

S

Shy, Spook—The way a horse deals with objects or sounds that frighten him. Shying is ducking sideways suddenly. Spooking is stopping, suddenly, then reacting. It is difficult and unpleasant to ride a spooky horse.

Snaffle—A mild bit that is broken in the middle. The fatter the snaffle, the milder its action.

Stallion—An ungelded (unneutered) adult male horse. Usually difficult to handle.

Stocking—A color term used to describe a leg that is white up to the knee (in front) or the hock (in back). See parts of the horse diagram.

T

Tack—The name given to the collection of stuff that goes on a horse. Saddle, bridle, girth, etc. May also be used as a verb, to mean putting all the stuff on to the horse.

Thoroughbred—A breed of horse known for its long graceful limbs and athletic ability. Thoroughbred horses are used in horse racing.

U

Untack—The act of removing the saddle and bridle from a horse.

W

Weanling—Colts and fillies who are between six and twelve months old. Most horses are removed from their mothers (weaned) at six months. At twelve months of age they are referred to as yearlings.

Welsh Pony—A lovely hardy breed of pony that originated in Wales (a small country next to England).

Whicker—Similar to nicker.

A Sneak Preview
of Book Two in the Sonrise Farm series

Stolen Gold

Sometimes when Jen was very busy—which was nearly always these days—she didn't have time to think. Today her thoughts demanded attention. They flooded her heart and soul, taking her breath away with wonder. *What if Mom had not helped buy Sunny, where would the horse be now? Where would she be?* "There are no coincidences in life," Jenny whispered to Sunny. "We are meant to be together."

Jenny thought about Sunny's registration papers. She had telephoned the Jockey Club two days ago. They had taken all of Sunny's information including the tattoo number on her upper lip. Jenny was looking forward to researching Sunny's bloodlines. Surely she must have a famous Thoroughbred in her ancestry; perhaps Secretariat or Man O' War. The papers would be delivered soon, maybe today!

She slid off Sunny's side and untacked her. The mare held her face low, to allow Jenny to slide the leather halter over her nose. Sunny released a noisy snort from her nostrils as she relaxed under Jenny's hand. Her eyelids drooped as she dozed in the sun.

Then suddenly Sunny's eyes snapped open. Her head jerked up and she stared at the empty driveway. Every muscle was taut and Jen could *see* her mighty heart pounding. "What's wrong, girl?" asked Jenny soothingly. She looked down the driveway but saw nothing.

Sunny reared. Jenny quickly unsnapped the safety clip at the mare's halter. *What is wrong?* she wondered, reaching for Sunny's halter. The mare went up again, wheeling on her hind legs in the same motion. She exploded into the air, sending up a spray of gravel. The big horse cleared the five-foot gate by a good eight inches.

Jenny watched Sunny as she streaked to the far end of the ten-acre pasture and melted into a stand of cedars. Jen's cheek stung and she touched it gently. Her fingers were wet with blood. Sunny's hasty departure had catapulted a sharp stone at Jenny's face. "Thank goodness it wasn't my eye," she whispered to herself, wiping the blood on her pant leg.

Angry dark clouds rumbled in, hiding the sun. *Could an approaching storm make Sunny crazy?* Jen wondered, rubbing her bare arms against the sudden chill. Then she heard the gravel crunch as a cavalcade of cars approached. The first car was the Thomas family station wagon, followed closely by a blue Mercedes Benz and three black Ford sedans. Jenny saw her dad's anguished expression, and the hair on the back of her neck stood up. Mom walked toward Jenny, her cheeks wet with tears.

What is going on? Tell me! Did someone die? She wanted to scream. Her cheek stopped stinging. Her lungs were having trouble taking in air. Was her heart beating? Yes, she could feel it pounding, galloping away.

A uniformed chauffeur opened the back door of the Mercedes and a tall, sharp-featured woman emerged. She looked around Sonrise Farm, her face frozen in anger. She was attired in wide jodhpurs and high black riding boots. She held a riding crop in her right hand and it swung with each step.

Two official looking men appeared out of the black Ford. They flipped their badges and introduced themselves as deputies.

Jenny clutched the rail of the fence helplessly. She didn't know what was going on, but every instinct was shrieking at her to climb on Sunny and get away.

"Where is she?" the woman demanded, rudely waving the deputy aside.

"Where is who?" boomed Mr. O'Riley, miraculously appearing behind Jenny.

"My horse, you idiot!" shrieked the woman.

"Get off my property," retorted Mr. O'Riley, pointing the way.

"I'm sorry sir, we have a warrant," said the older deputy. "It seems that you are in possession of stolen property. We have come to seize one Palomino mare named Gold N' Fire."